PASSPORT,
PLEASE

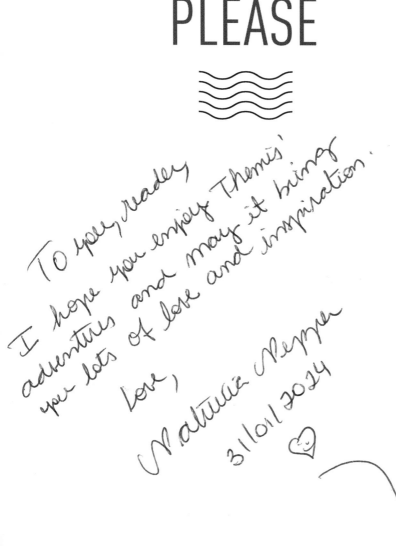

To every reader,
I hope you enjoy Themis'
adventures and may it bring
you lots of love and inspiration.

Love,
Matilda Pepper
31/01/2024

PASSPORT, PLEASE

	Pepper, Patricia, 1973 -
P424p	Passport, please. / Patricia Pepper; Illustration Yan Pinheiro; Translated by Mimi McQuaid.
	1. ed. -- London: Visto à Vista LTD, 2020.
	v.1. - Flight of the Phoenix. 244 p. : il. , p&b ; 23,4 x 15,6 cm
	Translation of: Passaporte, por favor.
	ISBN 978-1-8380161-1-1
	1. Brazilian literature. 2 .Immigration – Fiction
	3. Immigration – personal narrative. I. Title.
	CDD (21. ed.) 869.3

Book Design: Eduardo Venégas.
Catalog sheet: Daiane da Silva Martins Tomaz CRB14/622.
Illustration: Yan Pinheiro.
Proofreading: Andrew James Pepper and Papertrue.
Translation: Mimi McQuaid.

 The rights of this edition are reserved to Visto à Vista Ltd.

🌐 *Website: www.vistoavista.co.uk*   ✉ *E-mail: patriciapepper@vistoavista.co.uk*
📘 *Facebook: @vistoavistaoficial*   📷 *Instagram: @paty_pepper*

A CIP catalogue record for this book is available from the British Library.

PASSPORT,
PLEASE

PATRICIA PEPPER

VOLUME 1
FLIGHT OF THE PHOENIX

LONDON 2020

VISTO À VISTA LTD

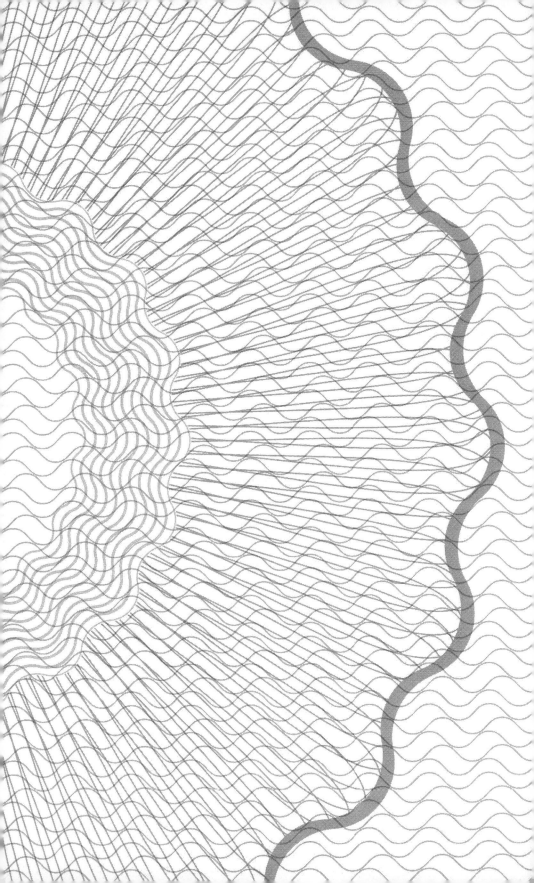

Background

In my memories of growing up, my mother always had a smile on her face. No matter what was happening around her, be it at home or in the outside world, she was, and still is, a happy person. Although she never went to school, she is, without a shadow of a doubt, one of the wisest people I have ever known, with an unshakeable inner strength. I like to think that I have inherited her way of dealing with life. Over the course of my personal journey until this day, there have been many times when I have had to muster my courage and confront head-on the challenges life threw at me. The bad experiences I have had along the way gave me the opportunity to learn and the strength to continue, even at times when it was not easy to do so. However, the more difficult the road was, the more determined I have been. At all decisive moments in my life, this determination drove me to take the next step – ever onwards and upwards.

I wrote this book to share with you, dear reader, what life has shown me: that it is possible to reach your goals even if the obstacles seem innumerable and insurmountable.

Two thoughts come to my mind: The first is one of several definitions I have come across of the word 'FAITH', beautifully explained here by Jack Canfield, an American author whom I greatly admire.

'Think of a car driving through the night. The headlights only go a hundred to two hundred feet forward, and you can make it all the way from California to New York driving through the dark, because all you have to see is the next two hundred feet. And that's how life tends to unfold before us. If we just trust that the next two hundred feet will unfold after that, and that the next two hundred feet will unfold after that, your life will keep unfolding. And it will eventually get you to the destination of whatever it is you truly want, because you want it.'[1]

If we can just believe that the rest of the road is there, even if we cannot see it, and carry on with our journey, we will reach where we want to be sooner or later. The important thing is to know where that is and to put the correct coordinates into our navigation device. Even if the road is closed – there may have been an accident – and we have to take an unexpected diversion, we must do so in the knowledge that this alternative route will still get us there.

---

1 Byrne, R. (2006). *The Secret.* Beyond Word Publishing, p. 57.

I arrived in the United Kingdom in 2001, and in 2008, I attained my dream of becoming an immigration officer. In the seven long years that separate these two dates, did the thought of giving up cross my mind? Yes, sometimes. However, in those moments of weakness, I would remind myself of how far I had come, how hard I had fought to reach that point, and I would focus on the final outcome rather than on the immediate obstacles in my path.

My second thought comes from Brazilian author Paulo Coelho, in my opinion, one of the best writers of all time:

'...To realise one's destiny is a person's only real obligation. All things are one. And, when you want something, all the universe conspires in helping you to achieve it.'[2]

In essence, three elements are necessary to reach one's goal: belief, desire, and the ability to make it happen. The ultimate success of the enterprise is up to you, and you alone.

Patricia Pepper
Spring 2020

---

2 Coelho, P. (1993). *The Alchemist.* Harper Collins, p. 23.

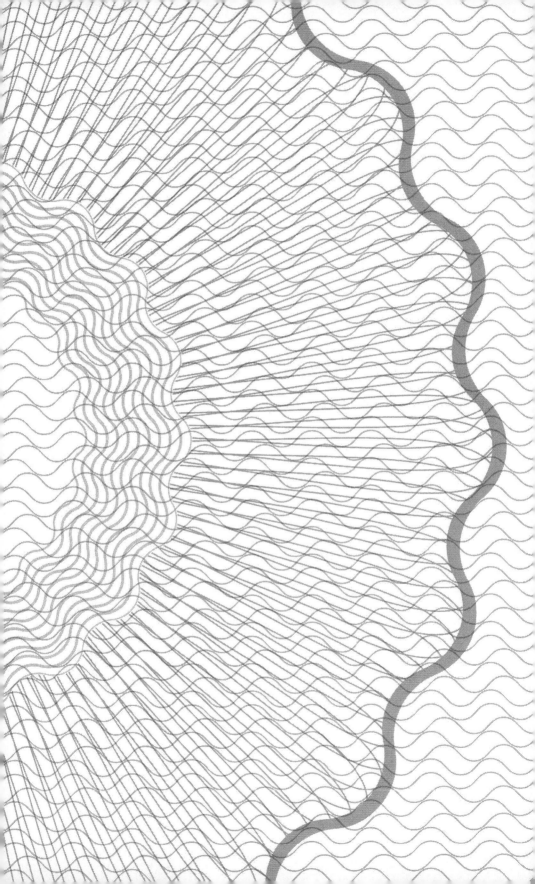

Dedication

This book is dedicated to my son, Arthur, whom I love infinitely.

Thanks

To my parents Nair and Armando *(in memoriam)*, my sister Silvana, and my brother Marcelo, for teaching me the real meaning of family.

To Sônia, my personal coach, for encouraging me to start writing.

To the British immigration service, for carrying on with its dedicated and tireless work.

To the United Kingdom, for being my home for the last 20 years.

To my team - Andrew, Daiane, Eduardo, Mimi and Yan - for working immensely hard on this project.

To immigrants all over the world, regardless of the reasons that led them to leave their homes, for continuing to make your contribution and working hard.

Finally, to all my family members, friends, clients, and followers on social media for, directly or indirectly, contributing to my story.

An army can go a hundred years without being used, but it cannot go a minute without being prepared. (Ruy Barbosa)[3]

Success is not final, failure is not fatal: it is the courage to continue that counts. (Winston Churchill)[4]

Whatever the mind can conceive, the mind can achieve. (W. Clement Stone)[5]

3, 4 e 5 PENSADOR. Available at: <https://www.pensador.com/frase/ODk0OTU4/> Acessed on 27/09/2020.

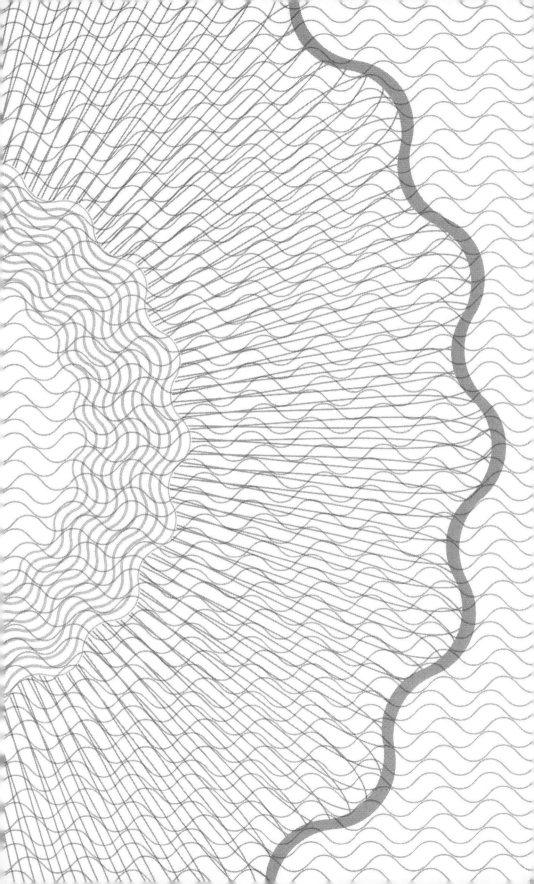

Summary

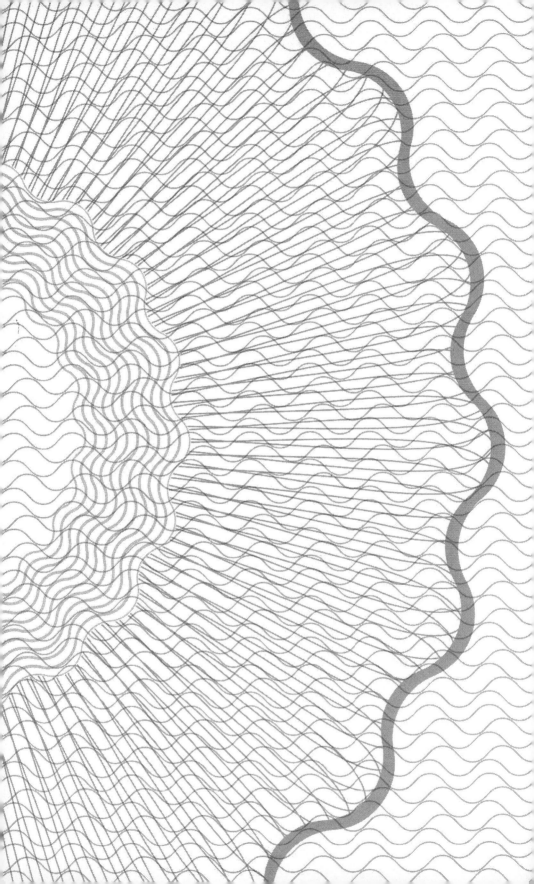

Introduction

DURA LEX, SED LEX – IT IS HARSH, BUT IT IS THE LAW

This book recounts a period in the life of Themis, a young Brazilian woman from Rio de Janeiro, who loves the sea, the sun, and the beach. However, when certain unexpected events create a devastating impact on her life, she decides to leave her world behind, exchanging the blue skies and the glittering beaches of Rio for the grey, mysterious gloom of London. She shares with us her journey as an immigrant in the United Kingdom and her progression from a supermarket checkout operator to a British civil servant, starting out as an assistant in the Tax Administration Department and rising to the rank of an immigration officer, working for Immigration and Border Control at one of the busiest airports in the world.

Between flashbacks that tell us more about her early life, the adversities she has faced, and the joy and pain of starting a new life in a new country, Themis takes us behind the scenes of the renowned British immigration system. Her light-hearted, entertaining, and, at times, dramatic narrative makes us laugh one minute and reflect on people's characters the next. Her stories also encourage us to think more deeply about the human aspects of her work – the personal conflicts and ethical dilemmas she encounters while executing her challenging, yet essential job.

It does not take long for Themis to realise that her new job as an immigration officer will involve a lot more than just checking documents at passport control. She has to go through a strict training procedure and, in a very short span of time, hone her powers of discretion. Her work naturally requires her to strictly adhere to the guidelines of the British immigration regulations, besides demanding a high degree of professionalism and a knowledge of the law. And all of this must be balanced with a certain amount of empathy – after all, the immigrant Themis once passed through passport control herself.

We see Themis struggle to reconcile these apparent contradictions in her new life. She is now an immigrant policing immigrants; she understands that her job is to uphold the law, but, at the same time, she cannot help but feel compassion for her fellow immigrants. She feels sad witnessing dreams of a better life shatter into pieces; she is thoroughly disappointed by the extent to which humans are prepared to lie and deceive. Above all, however, she becomes wiser, even if this wisdom comes at the cost of the dismantling of her youthful illusion as her eyes are opened to the very best – and, at times, the very worst – of human nature.

Weaving together intriguing storylines based upon the author's real-life experience, Themis takes us behind the screens that separate us from the inner workings of the airport. She gives us a glimpse into areas that usually remain inaccessible to the general public, such as the 'watch house', the 'pan', and the holding room. The reader experiences an insider's view of how the service operates – what happens when a passenger is stopped by immigration and left to 'simmer', the common tricks used to try and hoodwink immigration officials, and the procedures adopted to refuse entry to those who do not fulfil the strict criteria for admission and residence in the United Kingdom.

An organised country needs rules in order that its citizens enjoy a decent and dignified quality of life. The economy must be protected, and populations must be planned. It is precisely for the purpose of ensuring this order that immigration officers exist. They act as gatekeepers, and often find themselves in challenging situations. They need to draw upon their experience and gut feeling when scrutinising a case at hand, often needing to ask personal, occasionally embarrassing, questions. It's a tough job, but someone has to do it!

Prologue

Pandora's Suitcase

It was a September morning in 2001 when Themis decided to change her life. She had travelled to the 'Land of Hope and Glory' in July that same year, but she was going to settle there for good this time around. It was merely a week after the terrorist attacks on the World Trade Centre in the United States, and the world was still shaken to the core from having witnessed one of the biggest atrocities to affect humanity in generations. Despite the fear and misgivings looming in the air, the dominant emotion at that moment was one of hope. The world had watched, live, the events that unfolded to show the capacity of the human mind at its very worst. But wherever there is evil, there is also good. Numerous accounts of the heroic actions of those who responded to pleas for help, of people helping strangers, made it absolutely clear that the human race was not ready for extinction just yet. This was the prevailing feeling at that time. The domain of air travel and airport security would never be the same again, and it was in such times that Themis arrived at her new home.

The heightened airport security was security was evident as she boarded her plane in Lisbon. The atmosphere was one of fear. And Themis, too, was fearful of many things: would she be able to get work? How would she adapt to the new country? What about the weather? The food? Would she miss her family and friends? Could she do this? Above all, would she find the happiness she was looking for? Themis could not answer any of these questions. The one thing of which she was certain, however, was the presence of one male passenger at the entrance to the aircraft who was wearing an impressive and extremely elegant turban! Like her, the reaction of the other passengers was to pretend, albeit irrationally, that he was not even there. It is amazing how the human mind goes into a state of automatic self-defence when immersed in an atmosphere of fear, which leads to mistrust, whether deserved or not. *Had to be my flight, didn't it?* She was relieved when the flight arrived at its destination, but little did she know that this was only the beginning of a sequence of events that was about to unfold at the airport – events that would, while addressing some of her doubts, change the course of her life forever.

'Passport, please. Where have you come from today? Are you travelling alone?'

'Lisbon. Yes, it's just me', replied Themis.

'Thank you, and welcome to the United Kingdom', said the immigration officer.

Themis noted the presence of several armed police officers in the airport, making the place look like a battlefield. There seemed to be more security officers around than actual passengers. *I bet they stopped the guy in the turban,* she thought, breathing more easily now that she had arrived at her destination.

'Where have you travelled from, young lady?' asked the customs officer.

'Lisbon', replied Themis.

'We need to take a look at your suitcase. Are you carrying any animal products?'

'No'.

'Are you carrying anything that isn't yours?'

'No'. *I barely managed to fit all my own stuff in,* she thought. *I wouldn't have had any space for anyone else's things anyway.*

Themis noticed that the label from her original flight from Brazil was still attached to her case. This was perhaps why she was being asked so many questions.

'Open up your case, please'.

'No problem', she smiled, thinking, *What a pain!*

Themis watched as the officer pulled out her belongings from the suitcase and carelessly scattered them over the inspection desk. She had packed everything so carefully, and she could now see her underwear spread out over the desk, for the entire world to examine! *Good job I didn't bring those old ones, full of holes, that I like wearing at home,* she thought to herself. She was not really embarrassed, just a bit annoyed at the blatant lack of care shown toward her things. When he had finished emptying the case, the officer picked up a brush with a long head and what looked like a sticking plaster on the end. For a split second, Themis' mind was filled with horrific thoughts of where he was possibly going to stick it, but she relaxed once she saw him passing the brush over the lining of the suitcase. *God, what a relief!* She found it funny but managed to stop herself from smiling. *He's just checking for drugs.*

While the customs officer proceeded with his inspection, Themis took in the atmosphere and observed how the airport workers went about their tasks. When he had finished, seemingly annoyed at not finding anything of interest, he simply pushed all of her belongings to one side.

'You're not going to put all of that back in?' asked Themis.

'That's your job', he replied curtly.

This guy is a total arsehole, Themis thought, but thanks to him, she got the opportunity to hang around the area for a while longer as she gathered all her clothes and arranged them in her suitcase once more. Something about this environment fascinated her, and she decided right there and then that she would work at the airport one day.

'One of these days, I'm going to be here, working with you', she said to the customs officer, as he walked off to find his next victim, silently smirking in derision. Maybe he thought she could never make this dream come true or that she just wanted to distract him with her comment.

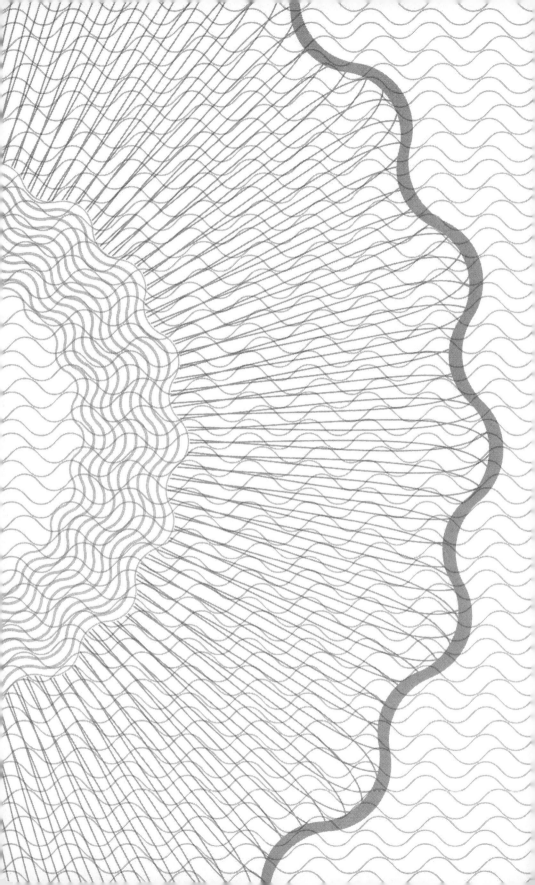

CHAPTER 1

The Queen's House, the Clock, and the Beatles Street

For Themis, one of the best things about working the first shift of the day during the summer was watching the sun coming up. With the "autopilot" switched on, Themis drove to the airport. The dawn brought back vivid memories of the blue sea at Leme: beach vendors selling iced tea and *biscoito de polvilho*, Rio's traditional beach snack, the feeling of salt on her body after spending a sunny day at the beach, and, more than anything, that atmosphere, so very familiar, but so, so far from her current reality. Now, proudly wearing her immigration officer's uniform as a mark of what she had achieved, Themis was on her way to her first day at work. The six long weeks of training were over, and the role-playing with actors during the training course would now be replaced with real-life situations and actual people.

'Good morning. I'm going to be your supervisor and mentor for the next few weeks', said Balder. 'We need to get a move on. The first flight of this shift is about to land'.

Everything felt calm at that moment. Three officers were taking their seats at fixed points where they would be spending the next hour. The chief immigration officer for that shift had already assumed his position at the watch house, a type of control room from where everything and everyone were visible and decisions – sometimes extremely difficult ones – were made.

'So, how long have you been working in this field? And what made you decide to come to the airport?' asked Balder.

'I started working for immigration four years ago, but I found the work boring. I mean, there's no fun in working with just documents and forms, is there?' said Themis. 'After a while, it all becomes very automatic. I needed something a bit more challenging, and I think working here with clients will make all the difference. I imagine that any questions about the process can be cleared up by directly asking the passengers instead of having to send them letters asking for documents, which was how we were required to do it when we were deciding on visa applications sent to us electronically or by post'.

'Absolutely right!' said Balder. 'I mean, what's the point of refusing entry to a passenger from a distance? Oh, and for the record, we're not dealing with clients here. We're not providing them with any kind of service. We're working for the British government! Look at the passengers waiting for their arrival checks. What do you see?'

'Passengers coming back from holidays, coming to do business, visiting their families?' replied Themis with a nervous smile.

'Every single one of those people is a liar until they prove to us that they're not!' said Balder, a more serious expression on his face this time around. 'You see that passenger there, at the back of the arrivals hall? Look, he's filling in his landing card. Look at the way he behaves. That passenger there is going to be your first refusal. Exciting, isn't it?'

'What do you mean, Balder?' snapped Themis. 'The guy's done nothing wrong. No, I'm not going to refuse anyone entry without a good reason. No way!'

'He's not done anything wrong... yet!' sneered Balder. 'Don't worry, we don't refuse anyone without a good reason. You're going to learn that the devil's in the detail. In this job, you'll soon see that it's the small things that make all the difference. Look at this guy, for example. He's already thrown at least half a dozen landing cards into the bin. For "normal" people, that might not mean anything, but not us – not the immigration rats. He's nervous. Wait here a moment; don't move'.

All Themis could think about was the comfortable decisions she used to make, from a distance, without suffering. If she refused someone a visa application, they could always make another application or even appeal the decision. *What about now though?* The arrivals hall was full of people. Officers were at their positions, vigorously stamping passengers' passports; some of them asking questions, others waiting for an interpreter's assistance to make communication with the passengers possible. Waiting in queues, those people were carrying their dreams, desires, and ambitions in their luggage – a hope for better times, away from their countries of birth, far from the place they had once called home.

'Here he is', said Balder with an air of satisfaction. He had brought the passenger he was talking about to Themis' desk. 'Speak to him in Portuguese. He can't speak any English'.

'What is the purpose of your journey?' asked Themis, looking at Balder, not particularly in agreement with what he had just said.

'*Não falo inglês*', said the passenger, confirming that he did not, indeed, speak any English.

A faint smile played at the corner of Balder's mouth, but he remained silent.

'What's the purpose of your journey, young man?' Themis politely asked, this time in Portuguese, as she examined his passport.

'Holiday', he replied. 'You speak Portuguese. Cool!'

Themis checked the passenger's passport details on the borders and immigration control system and noted that he had an adverse immigration history. This could mean any number of things, but something stood out in this case. The young man in front of her had had problems with a previous visa application.

'Ask him if he's ever had a visa refused in the past', Balder impatiently said as she finished reading the alert message on the system. 'I bet you a tenner he'll deny it and swear on his grandmother's life that he doesn't know what you're talking about!'

The message was telling her that this passenger had been refused a student visa less than a month ago. However, he was no longer travelling with the same passport he had used for the previous application, and as such, there was no record of this history in the travel document he was presenting her with now. It was customary practice for officers to write the number of the visa application on the last page of the applicant's passport, and if his visa had been refused, this number would be underlined.

'Balder, how did you…', said Themis. She then turned to the passenger and carried on with the initial interview questions: 'Have you ever faced any problem while applying for visas, either for the United Kingdom or any other country?' she asked him.

'No, never', he replied, not even blinking.

'Ask him if he knows anyone here', said Balder. 'And I don't think I even need to tell you that I already know the answer!'

'Do you know anyone here?' Themis asked.

'No, no', the young man replied. 'I've just come for a few days, on a holiday'.

'So, why England?' pressed Themis. 'Why didn't you choose some other country? One where you can speak the language, for example?'

'Ah, because this place is cool, and it's been my dream to visit here since I was a child', he answered. 'I always dreamed of seeing the clock and the Queen's house and the street the Beatles crossed'.

'Tell this fool to sit down', said Balder. 'In time, you're going to see that people who aren't telling the truth generally fall into this pattern. First, they don't know anything about the destination they intend to visit. If it has been his dream since he was a kid, you'd expect him to at least know that the big clock is called Big Ben, the Queen's house is Buckingham Palace, and the bloody Beatles street is actually called Abbey Road!'

'OK Balder, calm down', said Themis, trying to defuse the situation. 'That doesn't make him a liar though, does it? You haven't even given him a chance to defend himself'.

'Themis, I'm afraid you're going to be very disappointed in your fellow humans', said Balder. 'That perfect world you think you know, it doesn't exist. Since I began this job, I have stopped trusting even my own shadow! By the end of this shift, you'll be on your way to understanding this. At least I hope you will! You just watch. The Themis after working for the immigration service will be completely different from the one before you started here. Anyway, back to work. Come with me. I want to show you something'.

The two officers left the young man in the reserved waiting area, sometimes referred to as the 'pan', as they made their enquiries.

'Let's make a phone call', suggested Balder.

'To whom?' asked Themis. 'Buckingham Palace?' she added ironically.

'Oh, you're funny', said Balder. 'No, someone far more interesting than that'.

Balder put the call on speakerphone so Themis could hear the conversation. It rang a few times before a woman answered, 'Hello, information desk, how may I help you?'

'This is Officer Balder, calling from immigration. Could you put a call out for me please?' asked Themis' mentor.

'Of course', replied the woman. 'What do you need me to say?'

'Please ask if there's anyone waiting for a passenger called Felipe da Silva, arriving from São Paulo on flight PP8084', Balder instructed the receptionist.

'If anyone turns up, let me know and I'll come down to you'.

'No problem, Mr Balder'.

As they waited for the call from the information desk, the two officers printed out all the information on the passenger's record, in particular, a copy of the student visa application form that had been refused, together with the reason for its refusal. The passenger had no idea about what was going on behind the scenes as he waited for the security checks to be carried out in the reserved area, alongside others who were also left to 'simmer'.

It's like waiting in the wings for a theatre performance, thought Themis. The script, the costumes, the scenery – but here, someone's future depended on the behind-the-scenes production.

Themis' thoughts went back to the time she had dreamed of being in her present position. She had newly arrived in the United Kingdom and was serving at the head of a never-ending queue of a fast food restaurant. She didn't know much about the money, the culture, or the people, but she knew that, one day, she would be working on the other side of the street, at the Home Office, the headquarters of which were directly opposite the shopping centre where she worked. Her heartbeat quickened every time she saw someone in the queue wearing the ID badge bearing the British Crown. How she would love to wear that pass one day – maybe even work at the airport!

'Themis, I want to see these metal cupboards shining before we close for the day', ordered the manager. 'I want you to see your white face reflecting in the doors'.

Seven years later, those words still ate at her soul. She knew it had not been easy for her in the beginning, but that was just how it was for immigrants in countries far away from their homelands. When she mentioned to one of her co-workers that she would be wearing a badge bearing the British Crown one day, her colleague mocked her, reminding her that people like them did not get to work in those government positions, because they were nothing more than immigrants.

As these memories crossed her mind, Themis experienced a moment of sadness, but then she remembered that merely three years after those difficult beginnings, she had been successful in her application to join the civil service and began working in that same government department. In time, she had been invited to attend that very building, there, on the other side of the road – the building that, once upon a time, had been nothing more than an oasis in her imagination.

On her first day of work there, she had thought she would just be there for training. The manager asked her to go to the security office to have a photo taken for her ID badge. Placing that pass around her neck gave Themis a great feeling of encouragement and also the certainty that justice had finally been served. She then went on to work there, in that oasis, for four more years before she began work at the airport. On that first day of her new job, Themis crossed over the road at lunch time and went into the shopping centre. She walked past her old workplace and saw that everything inside was just as it used to be: the same workers who did not believe in their own potential and the same manager who had bullied her so badly. It was as if no time had passed at all.

Themis left her reverie as a message came over the internal tannoy system:

'Officer Balder, please come to the watch house. A call is waiting for you', announced a voice.

Themis looked sceptically at Balder. She could not believe it could be someone from the information desk outside the terminal.

'Yes, this is Balder', said the officer. 'Felipe's girlfriend? We're on our way'.

'Come on, come on', Balder impatiently urged Themis, grabbing his interview notebook and a ballpoint pen with the lid missing. 'Put your personal stamp in your locker. We can't take that through security to the other side of the terminal'.

They passed through security and travelled down the escalator to the first floor. Arriving at the information desk, they found a young woman waiting for them.

'Good morning. We're from immigration, and we'd like to know if you're waiting for someone?' Balder asked.

'Yes, that's right', the young woman replied. 'Felipe. He's my boyfriend. He's coming to stay with me here in the UK for about six months. I'm studying here, but he couldn't get a visa. Is he OK?'

'Felipe's fine', replied Balder. 'I just have a few routine questions for you', he said, looking at Themis and taking down every detail in his notebook. 'Does your boyfriend know that you're here at the airport, waiting for him?'

'He knows, yes', said the girl.

'Does Felipe have a job in Brazil?'

'No, he's unemployed at the moment, but his dad helps him out from time to time'.

'And how does your boyfriend think he's going to support himself here for six months? I mean, six months is a long time'.

'He's just coming to keep me company', she replied.

'Thanks for your help. We'll contact you if we need any more information'.

The jigsaw was starting to come together to reveal a picture, but a lot of pieces were still missing. Despite this, Balder appeared to be in no doubt as to how the case would end. He behaved as though he already knew everything there was to know about this young man.

Maybe he'd just got lucky? Yes, that must be it. How is it possible for someone just to look at a passenger from a distance and know all of that?

Once they were back at the terminal, delayed after getting stuck in an infernal queue behind the crew of an Air India aircraft, Balder and Themis went to the passenger arrivals area and retrieved Felipe from the pan.

'Just to make me feel better, can I ask him again what he came to do here?' asked Themis, still struggling to come to terms with Balder's verdict on this young man.

'Ask whatever you think you need to. After all, you're the officer in charge of this case', Balder said encouragingly. 'When you've got a bit of experience in this job, you'll see how two or three questions are generally enough to know what sort of a person you're dealing with'.

'OK', said Themis, still somewhat unconvinced. 'Felipe, please tell me again the reason for your visit to the United Kingdom'.

'Tourism. I came for a couple of weeks to see the place', he stated once more.

'Do you have a return ticket to Brazil?' she asked him.

'Yes...', said Felipe, taking a crumpled piece of paper from the pocket of his jeans.

'And where are you going to stay?' she asked.

'In a hostel, but I only paid for a couple of nights', he replied, doing his best to convince Themis. 'In case I wanted to go and stay somewhere else'.

'Here we go!' Balder sceptically exclaimed. 'Same old story. Themis, please explain to this gentleman that he is detained as of now and that we're going to confiscate his passport and luggage for further enquiries. Fill in the IS81[6] form that explains the legal grounds that give these powers to immigration officers. But before we take him to the holding room, tell him that we need to see his luggage'.

'Felipe, we just need to check a few things regarding your journey to the United Kingdom', explained Themis. 'While we do that, we're going to ask you to wait in our internal waiting room, where you'll be more comfortable and can have something to eat

---

[6] 'Notice to a Person Required to Submit to Further Examination'; this document permits the detention of passengers in order to carry out further investigation.

and drink. First, though, we need to collect your luggage. How many bags did you bring with you?'

'Two', he replied.

'Two cases for a two-week holiday?' she asked.

'Yeah, I didn't know if it was going to be cold or not, so I thought it would be best to bring more clothes just in case I needed them', Felipe replied.

The two officers led him to the baggage hall, where his were the only suitcases still going around on the carousel. The other passengers on his flight had already gone through immigration checks and collected their belongings. A calm atmosphere had been restored to the terminal, at least until the arrival of the next plane. Felipe, though, was starting to show signs of discomfort at having been held there for so long.

On opening the cases, Themis and Balder were surprised at the number of chocolates and wrapped gifts stuffed into the pockets of the cases.

'We have to open these gifts for security purposes', explained Themis. 'Why have you brought along so many presents if you don't know anyone here?' she asked.

'Erm... I... well...', said Felipe, confused. 'I might meet up with my cousin. She lives in Europe', he offered after a long moment of hesitation.

'Ah', said the officers, looking at one another.

Returning to the second floor of the terminal, they led Felipe to the holding room – or, as Themis preferred to call it, 'the waiting room'. Once he was in there, the assistant immigration officers would take his fingerprints and photographs. These biometric details would then be entered into a database that would carry out a search of the British immigration system across the world. Any information related to an adverse history on the passenger's record, at any British port of entry or visa application post, anywhere in the world, would be there.

While the identification process was underway, Balder and Themis prepared to interview the passenger. They had already sent over the details of the situation to the chief immigration officer on duty and entered all the information into the system. They had also prepared a file containing all the information collected about Felipe so far – his arrival, the initial desk interview, findings in his luggage, and other observations that had been made, including the details of the interview with Maria, his girlfriend.

'Standard procedure is for the officer to speak with the passenger directly, in their own language. This is only permitted in cases where the officer – as is the case with you, Themis – has the authority and the appropriate linguistic qualification issued by the border agency', explained Balder. 'However, to make the conversation easier between the parties, we'll use an interpreter this time. That way, you won't have to translate everything for me while simultaneously making the case notes'.

'OK Balder', agreed Themis.

They arrived at the interview room in the holding area. Felipe was already waiting for them. It was a medium-sized room. Themis could see a cold drinks machine and another vending machine with crisps and snacks. There was a public payphone, a television, a toilet, and, at the back, three interview rooms. Outside, there were two security guards, who were responsible for taking care of security and providing assistance to the passengers. They recorded the times at which people went in and out, including officers, and provided microwaved meals to detainees who wanted to eat lunch or dinner while they were in the 'waiting room'. Just ahead of this area, there was another room where the detained passengers' bags were stored. Balder asked one of the security guards to open the door so Themis could take a peek inside.

'It's like the suitcases are alive in here', laughed Balder.

'What do you mean?' asked Themis.

As they opened the door, they were met with a cacophony of beeps and buzzes from various mobile phones. These, no doubt, were calls from the detainees' relatives, friends, partners, and bosses, who were waiting outside and wanted to know what was going on. Those who got in touch with immigration would be given the number of the public payphone in the holding room, and this was the only way in which they would be able to contact their loved ones. Very often, a number of hours would pass before this contact was possible. This helped the officers, who preferred to speak to passengers before they contacted the people waiting outside for them. The credibility test was essential for the investigative work of the officers, who compared the responses given by all parties involved.

'Why aren't they allowed to keep their phones on them?' Themis asked somewhat naively.

'Unless you want your face and your identity broadcast live all over Facebook or YouTube, I don't think it's a great idea for us to let them have smartphones in there', said Balder, laughing. 'We only let them keep their phones if they don't have a camera. All detainees are searched before they go into the holding room, not just to see if they're carrying phones, but also to make sure that they're not hiding any pointed objects that could be used as a weapon against one of us'.

'Blimey!' exclaimed Themis. 'I hadn't thought about that'.

Even the Bic ballpoint pens were tied to the table and had their caps removed. Themis now understood why Balder always took the caps off his pens. All the tables and chairs in the room were screwed to the floor, and alarms and CCTV were installed all around the interview rooms for the safety of everyone. Balder told Themis that, on one occasion, a passenger had stabbed a pen into an officer's hand.

'Felipe, can you please come into the interview room with us?' Themis asked. 'Are you feeling OK? You understand the interpreter?'

'Yes', he replied.

'What is the purpose of your trip to the United Kingdom?' enquired Themis.

'I've already told you this several times!' he replied impatiently.

'I want you to tell me again', said Themis. 'We're formally interviewing you this time. Everything you say here will be recorded on your file. At the end of the interview, we'll make a recommendation to our chief immigration officer as to whether you should be granted permission to enter the country or refused entry. And I should point out that it is a crime to lie to an immigration officer. Do you understand everything I just told you?'

'Yes', said Felipe, somewhat calmer now.

Themis repeated her question.

'So, as I was saying, what is the purpose of your visit to the United Kingdom?'

'Tourism'.

'How long do you intend to stay?' asked Themis, writing down all the questions and answers on the passenger record sheet.

'Two weeks'.

'Do you know anyone in the United Kingdom, either British people or citizens of other countries?'

'No, no one', he said. 'I came on my own, and I'll stay on my own'.

'So, how do you explain the gifts and chocolate inside your case?'

'Like I said, they're for my friend who lives in Europe. She might come over to meet me here'.

Friend! thought Themis, incredulously. 'When we were looking through your suitcases, you told us that you had a cousin in Europe', she said. 'So, what is she, your friend or your cousin?'

'Well, to be honest, she's a friend, but we think of ourselves as cousins because we grew up together'.

'Have you ever made any type of visa application for the United Kingdom or any other country?'

'No', he replied emphatically.

'Are you sure?' Themis persisted. 'Are you categorically telling me that you have never applied for a visa to the United Kingdom?'

Themis found herself starting to agree with Balder. She was overwhelmed by a mixture of feelings. Sitting there in front of her was a fellow human being – someone from the same country as she – who was lying in a way that was almost convincing.

How can someone lie so openly – he's not even blinking – and worse, without feeling the slightest bit bad about it, thought Themis.

Up until this moment, she had really believed that Felipe would, at some point, own up to the whole thing and admit that he was actually there to meet up with his girlfriend, who was spending the year in the United Kingdom as a student.

'So, to sum up…', concluded Themis. 'You're coming to the United Kingdom, this is your first time outside of Brazil, you don't know anyone here, and you've come for a two-week holiday to see the Queen's house, the clock, and the Beatles street, right?'

Before Felipe could come up with another fabricated response, Themis opened his file in frustration and showed him a copy of the visa application he had made in Rio de Janeiro less than a month before. She also showed him a copy of his previous passport and a copy of the visa belonging to Maria, his girlfriend, who was waiting for him outside.

'So, who is Maria?' asked Themis, somewhat annoyed. 'And this passport here? Who's this, your doppelganger? And this student visa application with your signature on it, that's not yours I suppose? Look Felipe, I've defended you from the start. I really thought you were going to tell me the truth when we came in for the interview. But you've really let me down.'

'Well done, Themis', said Balder with pride in his voice. 'I think we've got our newest immigration officer in the terminal. I'm sorry if that was a bit difficult for you, but there'll be thousands more like him'.

'I didn't know that I had to tell you my girlfriend was here', said Felipe. 'I'm sorry if I didn't tell you the truth'.

'Felipe, unfortunately, I have to refuse you permission to enter on this occasion', said Themis. 'As I explained at the start of our interview, lying to an immigration officer is an offence. In addition to being refused entry, you'll be banned from entering the United Kingdom for the next ten years. Don't worry, we'll let Maria know of our decision. I'll give her the internal contact number so she can call you if she wants to'.

'Can you give her the gifts I brought for her?' he asked.

'Unfortunately, that isn't allowed for security reasons', explained Themis.

'We'll make the necessary changes to your ticket, and you'll be returned to Brazil on the next available flight. We'll be in touch with you again once we've spoken to our chief immigration officer. If you've understood everything, please sign here at the bottom of your interview notes. See you later'.

Themis and Balder left the room to take care of the paperwork necessary to send Felipe back to Brazil. They handed over the summary of the interview to the chief immigration officer and then called the airline company to inform them that a refused passenger would be returning to Brazil on the next flight that evening. Refused passengers always had priority seats. Even if the flight was fully booked, the airline was obligated to remove a checked-in passenger in order to make room for the detainee on board. Very often this led to bad feeling between airline workers and immigration officers; however, they were required by law to take the refused passengers. This was the main reason airlines required passengers to have return tickets, unless they held a valid entry visa for the United Kingdom.

Back in the changing rooms, Themis removed the insignia from her uniform and placed it in her locker, together with her personal stamp. Her first shift was coming to an end, and while she knew that she had done what she had to do, she could not help thinking about Maria, who must now be returning home alone. Felipe was on his way back to Brazil, having seen nothing of London other than the airport. He was going back to the same old life in the knowledge of one thing for sure: it would be a long time before he would be able to visit the Queen's house, the clock, and the Beatles street.

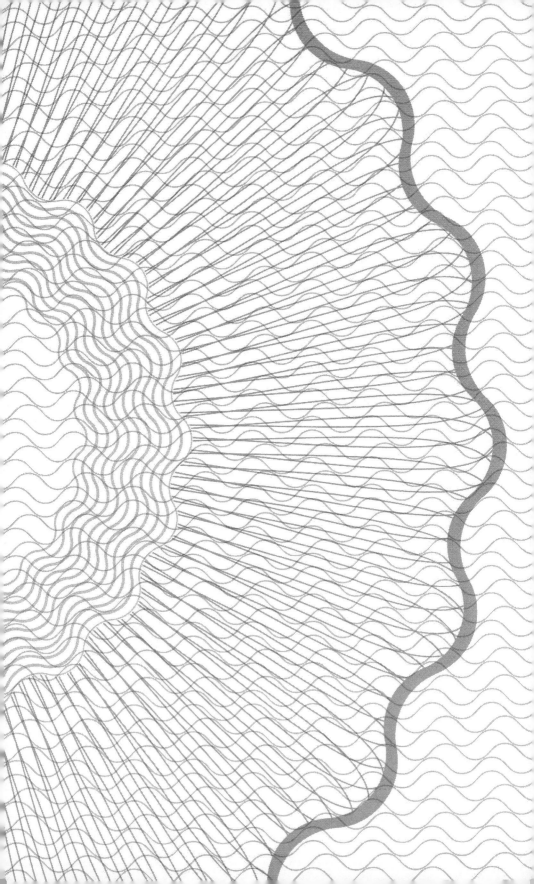

CHAPTER 2

A Waterfall of Nail Varnish

Hundreds of passengers were surging through the airport terminal, all at the same time. As security staff ran from one side of the terminal to the other, and intermittent tannoy announcements mixed with the deafening hubbub of people shouting and trying to communicate in different languages, Themis looked in despair at the hordes of people arriving. It was a portrait of a lawless land; there was no order – only fear and uncertainty. What did it all mean for the country's security? The economy would not be protected; there were nowhere near enough jobs for all these people who were trying to get in. What about public services? They would collapse! There would not be enough beds in hospitals or places in schools. Not enough police to contain the violent disorder that would almost certainly break out on the streets! Chaos looked inevitable! Without work, there would not be any money, and without money, no one would be able to buy food or have a house to live in. In the midst of all this turmoil, people would end up invading supermarkets to steal food. Some families might even be forced to sleep rough.

'Look! They're opening the gates!'

'No, you can't just come in like that! There aren't enough visas for everyone! No! No! Balder, Balder, Balder!'

Outside, heavy rain beat against Themis' bedroom window. Her breathing was laboured, and she was bathed in sweat. She looked at the ceiling as her eyes adjusted to the constant darkness, broken only by the lightning flashing outside. She sat up, realising that it had all been just a dream. Relieved, she looked at the time: 2:22 a.m. Since starting work at the airport, Themis had woken up at the same time every morning. Were these changes in her sleeping pattern the result of working shifts? Insomnia? Had she made a mistake at work?

No, she was still with her mentor, Balder, "the impeccable supervisor", she reminded herself. It had not escaped her notice that he was always very well groomed. Rather dishy, as her grandmother would have said. He had black hair, with the bluest eyes she had ever seen, always clean shaven and smelling good. He was over six-foot tall and clearly worked out at the gym. He brought in his uniform on a hanger every day, so it would not get crumpled on his journey to work. He kept his shoes so shiny that they looked like a new pair every day. His voice was soft, but his words cut like a sharp knife. He had started working with the immigration service soon after leaving school. Twenty years on, now aged thirty-eight, he was one of the most experienced officers at the airport. Themis had once asked him why he had never applied for any of the management vacancies, given he had so much knowledge. Her "impeccable supervisor" explained to her that he liked getting his hands dirty and could never see himself inside the watch house, supervising other officers, so far away from the action. He did not want to direct the show; he wanted to be the lead actor. In addition to this, he enjoyed training new officers and often joked that he needed to multiply the number of immigration rats who were just like him.

Damn! It's four a.m. already! Themis realised with a start. *I'm supposed to be starting at six!*

She jumped out of bed, and after a quick shower, set off for work. She had bought her house in Kent a year after her arrival in the United Kingdom, but her place was more than eighty miles away from the airport where she worked and the daily commute on the motorway was already starting to wear her down.

I must have slept badly last night, Themis thought to herself, trying to play down her tiredness. Until recently, she had never thought that she would be able to sit behind the wheel of a car. In 1997, she had lost her best friend in a traffic accident in Rio de Janeiro, and for the longest time, she could not contemplate the very idea of driving herself. She had not known just how far this was from the truth though.

As soon as she got through the application process to become an immigration officer, she realised her days of public transport were numbered.

How will I be able to do all these different shifts if I don't drive? When she started attending the officer training course, she also started taking driving lessons. She would never forget her first lesson with an English instructor.

'Right, Themis, so here we have the steering wheel, the clutch, the brake, and the accelerator. OK?'

This guy has got to be joking, she thought.

'Yep. OK. And where's the key?' she asked.

'Here it is'.

'Ah, yes. So, where do I go to switch this thing on? Inside the steering wheel? Outside?'

'What do you mean, Themis?' the instructor asked her, sounding slightly shocked. 'You do know it's on the outside, right?'

'Yes, of course!' replied Themis. 'See, the thing is, I've only got six weeks to learn to drive. I'll be finishing my training in six weeks, and after that, I'm going to have to drive to work'.

She remembered having to face her fellow officers when she came back to work after failing her first attempt at the practical test.

'How did you get on, Themis? Did you pass?'

Themis' expression was enough to tell them that the test had not gone well. She was unable to get into fifth gear on the main road.

I really messed it up, she thought.

The gears on the instructor's car were not exactly smooth at the best of times, and on the day of the test, the stupid thing had decided to get stuck. Themis realised that she was going to have to buy her own car, and this was where things started to get surreal! In the car showroom, whilst she looked at some models, the saleswoman explained the procedure to Themis, who then decided upon the car she would get. She wanted something economical, so the saleswoman suggested she bought what was, at that time, the latest Peugeot – the 308. Powerful, economical, and comfortable, it was exactly what Themis needed, as she did not relish the idea of spending a night at the side of the M25 with a broken-down car. When the time came to sign the paperwork, the saleswoman asked for her driving licence.

'Ah, yes, my licence. It's going to be issued next month', said Themis.

'What do you mean? Did you lose it?' asked the saleswoman.

'I didn't lose it, no. I've actually never had a driving licence in my life, but that's not important, is it? Next month I'll be passing my driving test, so I'll have my licence then'.

An uncomfortable silence filled the air. Themis was so confident she would pass the test that she did not realise just how ridiculous her words had sounded. She was about to buy a brand-new car without even having a driving licence. She had failed her first attempt at the practical test and did not know, if she was being totally honest, how many more attempts she was going to need before she passed – or even if she actually would! A few seconds went by before the saleswoman finally broke the silence. It had taken her a little time to absorb the bizarre situation before her: selling a car to a crazy woman who did not even have a driving licence.

'If it's OK with you, I'm just going to talk to my manager'.

A few minutes later, she returned and let Themis know that everything was fine, but that she would have to come back with someone who had possessed a driving licence for more than three years. 'No problem', Themis replied, and that was the end of it. Things often happened like this in Themis' life: she had never been great at making too many plans ahead of time. Instead, she resolved problems as they came up and did not waste a lot of her time thinking about what could go wrong.

I mean, what's the worst that could happen? If I don't pass the next time, I'll just have to put up with that instructor for another three weeks, not to mention three weeks of the other officers taking the piss! Oh yes, she really needed to pass the next time, come what may!

'Morning Themis. You OK?' asked Balder, spotting her having a coffee in the international arrivals area of the airport.

'I'm fine. Well, apart from my apocalyptic dream last night', she replied with a laugh. 'But yeah, we won't go into that. Hang on, I'm just finishing my coffee'.

The pair walked through security, to the Airside zone of the terminal. On arriving at the watch house, they had to sign the attendance book – although officers would usually leave a stamp rather than a signature in the book to indicate their presence. It was at this hour of the morning that some unwary worker would invariably get reprimanded by the chief immigration officer, usually at 6 a.m., after the night shift was almost over and having been in such a hurry to get out, for setting the wrong date on their stamp.

I've seen people put the date as 1008 instead of 2008, thought Themis. *I mean, back then Brazil – and its gold, to be more precise – hadn't even been 'discovered' by the Portuguese!*

She sometimes thought that her beautiful homeland would have ended up in a better shape if its future had been left in the hands of the indigenous *Tupiniquim* people. Instead, Brazil had been invaded and its people massacred by Europeans, who spent many years ravaging and ransacking the country, and the effects of the whip were still felt to the present day. The indigenous people offered little resistance to the white man who, besides inflicting upon them the diseases that he brought with him on his giant ships, enslaved, tortured, and forced his culture onto the original inhabitants of the country. A rather curious thing happened when the Portuguese forbade the entry of foreigners into Brazil during the colonial period. It was not until 1808, in the years leading up to Brazil's independence, that the stream of Europeans coming to start a new life in the country increased, and the country received Portuguese, Spanish, Swiss, German, English, Italian, and, later, Japanese settlers. The beloved homeland of Brazil was kind to her children – both native and adopted – looking to prosper in the New World or work on the cultivation of its immense coffee fields. Now, in the twenty-first century, the opposite phenomenon was being observed, as Brazilians were leaving their country to seek new lives in Europe. In present times, Europeans were not as eager to welcome their South-American cousins. These new Brazilians were the result of a mixture, in large part, of native Indians, white Europeans, and black African and Caribbean people.

'The Air France flight is on chocks. Everyone to their posts', came the alert from the chief immigration officer.

'Balder, are bosses always in a bad mood?' asked Themis.

'Not always. Most of them just stick a couple of officers in the watch house and go off to sleep in the back office. The sneaky gits set their alarms to wake up just before the six a.m. shift begins. The Dungeon Master's pissed off because he's one of the few people here who actually take responsibility and stay awake all night. He may even interview a passenger or two if he's feeling particularly animated. Do your job properly, and you won't ever have to see his bad side', warned Balder.

Passengers began to filter through. Most of them passed quickly through the European Economic Area (EEA) arrivals control, while a smaller number formed a queue in the area designated for travellers from outside the EU. Balder put out an announcement stating that their position was open.

'Hang on Balder, I haven't even got into the system yet!' cried Themis.

'No problem. We don't wait for them; they wait for us!' replied Balder.

Upon opening their positions, a woman, who looked about sixty-five, approached them.

'*Bom dia,* I don't speak English', she said politely.

'Not a problem, madam. My supervisor over here speaks Portuguese', said Balder, pointing towards Themis who was sitting next to him.

Balder spoke fluent Italian and decent Mandarin, which made him a great colleague to work with: In addition to his unquestionable knowledge and experience in matters related to the job, he was a first-rate linguist.

'Did you just promote me, Balder?' asked Themis, laughing.

'Not yet, Themis', replied Balder. 'I just said that because I have a feeling you're going to be soft on this passenger because of her age. Am I right?' He went on, 'Well, you're about to find out that rule number one, everyone here is a liar, has a second part. The passenger's age means nothing!'

'You scare me a bit when you talk like that', said Themis. 'Passport, please'.

'Yes, of course', replied the woman. 'Do you want to see my return ticket? And my travel insurance? I've got travel insurance too. My daughter's waiting for me outside. I'd love to see my granddaughter too, but she'll be on her way to school with her dad'.

'Just your passport is fine, Mrs Rodrigues, thank you', said Themis. 'How long are you planning to stay in the United Kingdom?'.

'It says on the ticket, dear', replied the passenger.

'You don't know how long you're going to stay here, not even a rough idea?' asked Themis, finding the answer a little strange.

'Yes, yes... two, three months... the same as always, dear'.

Themis examined the woman's passport and saw that she made the same journey every year, always in the summer. For the past five years, she had a single-entry stamp for each year she had come to visit her daughter.

'You come to the United Kingdom every year? Who lives here?' asked Themis.

'Yes, I come every year to stay with my daughter and her family. I stay for a few months and then I go home'.

'Themis, ask if her daughter's working here', interjected Balder. 'I would guess probably not, given that she's got a daughter of school-going age. If that is the case, I'd be very interested in finding out if it's the husband who pays for his mother-in-law's air ticket every year. That's what I'm curious to know'.

'Balder, please have a bit more respect', pleaded Themis. 'Do you really think she's coming over here to work at her age?' She was somewhat taken aback by Balder's suspicions.

'Themis, stay focussed'.

'So, Mrs Rodrigues, what does your daughter do here in England? Does she work?' asked Themis.

'No, no. My daughter stays at home', the lady replied. 'Only her husband works'.

'Bingo!' said Balder. 'Themis, do you really think a pensioner is going to have enough money to pay for international flights every year?' he asked her. 'Chuck her in the pan!'

'Eh? But why, Balder?' asked Themis, still not understanding.

'Come on, let's have a look in her luggage', ordered Balder.

The officers went to the watch house to tell the chief immigration officer what had taken place up to that point and the reasons behind their intervention. They then took the passenger to the baggage reclaim area.

'How many bags did you bring?' asked Themis.

'Three, dear', replied the elderly lady, finding this question a bit strange. After all, she came to the country every year and no one had ever stopped her before, never mind all the embarrassment.

Balder always liked to look through contents of the suitcases by himself. While he was checking the first one, Themis and an assistant officer examined the second one. Themis had some difficulty opening it because it was very full – probably well over the baggage limit.

'I think I've managed it', she said finally.

As she opened the case, a waterfall of nail varnish bottles spilled out and cascaded onto the table, some crashing down onto the floor. Themis did not react. She could not, after all, stop hundreds of bottles from falling.

'What on earth!' she exclaimed in shock.

'It's nail varnish, dear', replied the woman, who did not quite know where to look.

'Yes, I can see it's nail varnish', retorted Themis. 'My question is, why would you need so much nail varnish just for a holiday?'

'I like painting my nails', replied the woman, somewhat disconcerted.

Themis looked at Balder, not quite knowing what to make of everything in front of her. Balder returned her gaze with the same expression he had had on his face when he went to fetch the young man filling in his landing card at the end of the arrivals hall. That look, like the one when you find out who took the last chocolate biscuit...

Some of the nail varnish bottles smashed when they hit the ground, creating a rainbow of colour where they fell. The officers closed the suitcases and led the woman to the holding room. After the standard procedures had been carried out, she was left there to rest, as the officers examined their findings and made various other checks.

'I'm going to have a quick look at her Facebook page. What do you think, Balder?' asked Themis.

'I think that's an excellent idea. You can often find something useful there', Balder encouraged her.

Their work colleagues were watching the pair from a distance. Some came towards them and made jokes at their expense.

'Themis, what on earth is Balder teaching you? I didn't know that we were supposed to be stopping little old ladies coming to see their grandchildren'.

'Balder, take a look at this', said Themis, not believing what she had found. 'People will never cease to amaze me. Just when you least expect it, just when you think it's impossible to get it wrong, you discover something that turns everything upside down', she marvelled.

There, on the passenger's Facebook page, was the following announcement:

'*Hello my lovely clients! Ângela Rodrigues will soon be back in London, and she's bringing some*

amazing new colours to give you the most up-to-date nails around! Book now on 07987654321. Incredible offers available! Inbox me for more information.'

'Themis, check this mobile number. See if it's the same one she just gave us to call her daughter in London', asked Balder.

'It is!' replied Themis, amazed. 'Balder, when I grow up, I want to be just like you!'

Themis wondered if she would ever be half as good at her job as Balder was. He made everything seem so obvious, so easy. It was true that things were getting easier for her as her knowledge of the job increased, but she still doubted if she would ever get any pleasure or, even, job satisfaction from carrying out those difficult and, at times, challenging tasks on a day-to-day basis. She was not sure she would be able to deal with all the negative energy: a broken dream, a lie discovered, the rejection felt by an unfortunate passenger, the pain caused by a wound she had picked open – even if she did have the law on her side. Themis felt she was interfering with the passengers' destinies. These were not just a few broken bottles of nail varnish on the floor; they were broken dreams, a shattered rainbow of hope and happiness. It was her job to decide whether this passenger should have the opportunity to improve her life or whether she should go back from where she came. Still, Themis knew that her job was important, a job that had to be done – after all, there were good reasons for immigration into any given country being controlled. Protecting the economy and public services, promoting national security, preventing crime and the illegal entry of merchandise, to name but a few. Something that could appear innocent, like a person coming to the United Kingdom for a few months to work without permission, had far greater repercussions than the little money that they would earn. Informal workers took away work from those living legally in the country, and they did not pay taxes that would be used for public services. An increased offer of illegal work led to a lowering of wages, as consumers tended to seek out the lowest possible price for the services they required. Yes, it could seem insignificant when only one person was taken into consideration, but the large-scale impact was significant and damaging.

'Good afternoon. This is Officer Themis. Am I speaking to Amanda?'

'Yes, is my mum OK?' asked the passenger's daughter, who was waiting outside.

'Yes, she's fine. We just need to ask you a few questions about your mum's trip to the United Kingdom. Is that OK?' asked Themis.

PATRICIA PEPPER

71

'Yes of course, but is there anything wrong? Why has she been stopped?' asked the daughter.

'We're just asking for a little more information for the moment', said Themis. 'How long will your mum be staying in the United Kingdom?'

'Six months. She always comes and stays for that long, and we've never had any problems before'.

'Who paid for your mum's ticket?'

'She bought it herself. She used her Brazilian pension money'.

'How much pension does she receive each month?'

'About six hundred *reais* a month, but we pay for her food and cover her living costs while she's here'.

'Can I ask you if you are working at present? And what's your immigration status in the United Kingdom?'

'I'm not working at the moment. I have a five-year-old daughter who's in primary school. I'm married to an EU citizen'.

'Thanks for your help, Amanda. We'll get in touch again if we need to'.

'But how long are you going to keep my mum? She'll be tired... she's an elderly lady, and she's been travelling since yesterday'.

'Yes, we're aware of this. Don't worry, your mum's fine. Thanks again', said Themis, ending the call.

'So, you see my problem here, Themis?' asked Balder. 'This passenger has an income of just over a hundred pounds a month, which comes from her pension. There's no way she can afford to pay for an international air ticket every year and still survive in Brazil on that kind of money. So, in this case, given that the daughter doesn't work, it would be fair for us to assume that the passenger is going to have to work here in order to cover her costs. Otherwise, there's no way she'd be able to come to London for such a long time every year. The law on visiting the UK forbids work. We have to do this to protect the economy, amongst other things', he explained. 'I think you already know where all this is going – but before we make a decision, we'll have to interview her formally'.

Life is pretty tough for economic migrants, thought Themis. *In developed countries, the general idea is that retired people can enjoy their old age without having to worry about their financial situation, about how they're going to pay the rent, because they're very likely to have their own house. They don't have to worry about paying for medical treatment, because the State looks after their health. Or how they're going to pay for food and general expenses, because their pension contributions, taken from their salary over their years at work, are usually enough to cov-*

er all these. This is far from the reality in developing countries such as Brazil, she mused.

'Hi Mrs Rodrigues, we're here to interview you formally. We're going to ask you some questions about your visit to the United Kingdom. I must warn you that it's a crime to lie to immigration officers. After the interview, we'll pass on your case to our manager and then make a decision as to whether you can come into the country. Are you OK? Do you understand the interpreter?'

'Yes, I understand. I just don't know why I'm here', replied Mrs Rodrigues.

'You're here because we don't believe that you're a genuine tourist, and this is why we need to ask you some more questions. So, to begin with, what is your purpose for visiting the United Kingdom?'

'Like I said before, dear, I've come to visit my daughter, my granddaughter, and my son-in-law'.

'How long do you plan to stay?'

'That depends', replied the woman. 'Sometimes I stay for four, five, or six months. Never more than six months, though. Because I know that's the maximum allowed'.

'What do you do in Brazil? Do you work? Are you retired?'

'I'm retired, and I live with my son. My husband has passed away'.

'I'm sorry to hear that. Why hasn't your son come with you?'

'Ah, he couldn't afford the airfare. He's not working at the moment, you know. Life in my country is very difficult right now'.

'But if it's that difficult, Mrs Rodrigues, how do you manage to buy a ticket every year?'

'I put aside a little money here and there, and my daughter helps me as well'.

'But your daughter just told me that she isn't working at the moment. Where does she get this money to help you?'

'I don't know. I imagine her husband helps her out'.

'Do you work while you're in the United Kingdom?'

'What do you think? I can't even speak English'.

'We found a large amount of different nail varnishes as well as a manicure set in your suitcase. Why are you bringing along these objects if you're here as a tourist?'

'It's like I said. I like to do my nails, and I also do my daughter's nails. And her friends' nails'.

'We found this advertisement on your Facebook page. Did you write this post?' asked Themis, showing the woman a copy of the profile page that she'd printed out.

'Yes, I did', she admitted.

'And you know that, as a tourist, you're not

allowed to work in the United Kingdom, right? Every year when you come into the country, we stamp your passport as a visitor, and this stamp clearly states that while you're here, you may not work or claim benefits. On that basis, I'm afraid that we're going to have to refuse you entry on this occasion. I really am sorry. We'll let your daughter know that you'll be returning to Brazil on the next available flight'.

'But... I won't be able to see my granddaughter?'

'I'm afraid not'.

'Will I ever be able to come back again?'

'If your circumstances change, you'll be able to apply for a tourist visa from Brazil', said Themis. 'If you've understood everything, please sign here, at the end of the interview record'.

The officers left the holding room and walked towards the office to organise the removal of yet another passenger. Themis had thought that things would get easier with her work, but this refusal had made her very sad. She thought about the precious moments between grandmother and granddaughter that she had just prevented. The embrace that the woman would not be able to give her daughter.

What if something happens to her, she could not stop herself from wondering, *and this is her last opportunity to see her family?*

'Themis, you're doing really well!' said Balder, trying to lift her mood. 'See how confident you were in that interview? You know, I think you're ready to work alone now. Your supervised stage will be complete at the end of this week'.

'Thanks Balder, but I can't stop thinking about that family', Themis sadly said.

'I know Themis, but nobody said this job was going to be easy. Unfortunately, it has to be done – and you're doing it really well. Now, let's get a move on. The flight back to Brazil is in two hours, and we have a lot we need to do before then'.

'OK, I suppose you're right, Balder'.

Themis quickened her pace at the end of her shift. She did not want to miss the next staff bus that would take her to the car park. She wished to be on the road before the traffic started getting too heavy on the M25. She took her handbag from her locker and ran to the bus stop with Balder.

At the end of yet another working day, Themis felt this was the perfect job for anyone who did not like routine, as one day was never the same as the next. Officers never knew what story the next passenger would tell them when they arrived at their desks, but they had to be prepared at all times. After all, as Balder would say, it was up to the passengers to prove their innocence. In criminal law, the State had to prove, beyond all reasonable doubt, that the defendant was guilty. For immigration services, according to Balder, every passenger was a liar until they proved otherwise.

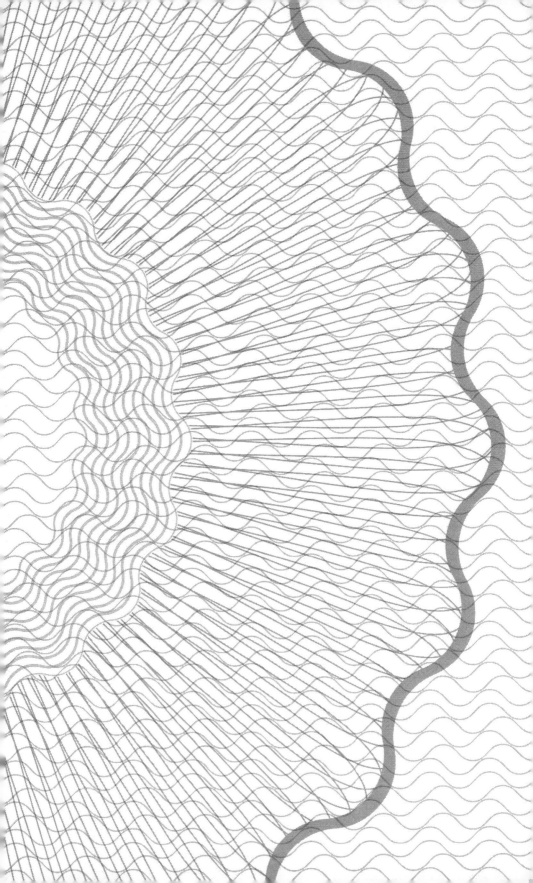

CHAPTER 3

The Rogue ID Card

2:22 a.m. Themis stared at the clock. She was no stranger to sleepless nights, but this one was somehow different. Something felt wrong, but she could not quite put her finger on what it was. She had left the terminal in a rush after her previous shift. Moreover, she was still thinking about the manicure lady who, as a result of her doing her job properly, would not get to see her granddaughter. Themis decided to get ready earlier than usual and do her make-up at home instead of in the airport carpark.

She liked sitting there, in her car, so close that she could smell the aviation fuel. The planes flew low over the airport workers' cars as they came in to land. Sometimes, Themis would sit and watch the traffic jam in the sky, particularly during the summer months, when the flow of passengers increased – as did the number of refusals, of course. Once her make-up was done, she would organise her bag, which usually contained plenty of fruit and a Marks and Spencer ready meal. She was not sure whether or not to put in a dessert as well. A few days earlier, an overzealous security officer had tried to stop her bringing mashed potato into the terminal, insisting that it was a form of liquid. It was only after serious negotiations that she had managed to save her lunch from the waste bin. Themis would then pick up her other bag, this one slightly smaller. She carried it with her when she was on duty at the desk. It usually contained her diary, mobile phone, some pens, and her personal landing stamp.

This morning she thought it felt a little heavier than usual, and as she opened it to take a look inside, her heart jumped: She had brought her personal stamp home with her the night before!

Oh God, no, she thought. No! What the... How many times has Balder told me I must NEVER take my stamp past security! I'm going to have to message him...Mayday, mayday, mayday!

Themis did not know whether to laugh or cry. She had recently read about how the codeword *'mayday'* for an emergency had been coined by a radio operator at Croydon Airport. This airport, just south of London, was no longer operational, but it was there that the British had pioneered the creation of early air traffic control systems. They also had built the first passenger terminal in the world, right there in Croydon, where her career in immigration began, in the big building opposite the shopping centre where she had worked in a fast food restaurant.

Come on, Balder, answer the phone, urged Themis.
Balder picked up.

'Morning Themis, everything OK?' he asked.

'Everything is definitely not OK, Balder. Something terrible has happened!'

'What is it, Themis? Whatever it is, we'll sort it out', he reassured her.

'I brought my personal stamp home by mistake! Remember how we left in a rush yesterday? What's going to happen? I'll get the sack, won't I?' asked a panicked Themis.

'Calm down. We'll talk once you get to the airport, OK? Speak to you in a bit'.

'But... but... Balder, Balder? Ohhh, he hung up!'

As she made her way into the airport, she could not think about anything except the stamp in her bag. *What if the alarm goes off when I walk through security? What if I get sent to prison? What if I get to see the Dungeon Master's evil side? Shit, shit, shit, shit, shit! I am in so much trouble! There's no way I'm even going to try to get my dessert in today. I can't risk attracting any more attention. Come on, Themis, focus,* she thought, trying to stop herself from panicking. She felt as though she was trying to smuggle illegal goods into the terminal.

Shoes – pass.

Belt – pass.

Bag – pass.

Phew. She had made it through security without any problems. She had imagined the customs dogs sniffing out the stamp and alerting their handlers as she went past them. *Themis, come on – it's made of metal! Focus, focus!*

She felt like she was back in primary school, about to face the head teacher. The United Kingdom had been the last country in Europe to abolish corporal punishment in schools. *Has it been abolished in the immigration service as well?* she wondered. *Who's in charge of the watch house today?*

'Morning Balder', she said, walking quickly. 'So, what are we going to do?'

'Themis, it's very simple', he explained. 'You either tell the truth and face the consequences, or you lie and face the consequences. The security chief immigration officer's job includes making random checks on staff lockers. Taking your stamp out of the terminal is technically viewed as serious misconduct, but you're still training, so I wouldn't worry too much about it. Anyway, I just looked in my locker and it doesn't appear to me that there was an inspection last night. It's your decision now'.

'I think I'd rather tell the truth, Balder. I don't like the idea of lying. I don't want to feel like one of those passengers we send back home', Themis said. Then she asked Balder, 'Who's in the watch house today?'

'Ian Gelos. He's also a security chief immigration officer', he replied.

When they reached the watch house, Themis approached the chief immigration officer. Balder remained in the doorway, watching Themis from a distance.

'Good morning, Mr Gelos. I've got a very serious confession to make', said Themis.

Balder laughed silently. He could see that she was terrified.

'It's... I took something home last night that I shouldn't have', said Themis.

'And what was that, Themis, Balder?' asked her superior, finding her discomfort highly amusing.

'No, my personal stamp. It was an accident'.

Mr Gelos and Balder could not contain themselves any longer and started laughing aloud at Themis.

'What's so funny?' asked Themis, her arm outstretched with palm upturned.

'Get out of here you two', said Mr Gelos, roaring with laughter. 'Just don't do it again, Themis. Otherwise, I'll have you writing out "I must not take my personal stamp home with me" a thousand times. Understood?'

'Yes, of course', replied Themis, and the two left the watch house.

'You were lucky there. Ian is pretty easy-going. He always sees the funny side', Balder told her.

'That was a close call!', said Themis, relieved that it was all over.

The immigration control area was already full of passengers. All the seats in the central control area were occupied by officers. Themis and Balder made their way towards the EEA control, where she was now able to deal with passengers on her own. Balder sat at another position, not far from Themis. The queues were long, but a passenger some distance away caught her eye, as he looked so different from the other people coming off the flight from Portugal. He was wearing a leather hat, with leather boots of the same colour, and a bag was slung across his chest.

With that outfit, all he needs is a big old knife and he'll look just like some historical bandit from the north-east of Brazil – no prizes for guessing where he's from! she thought.

'Passport, please. Where have you travelled from today?' asked Themis.

'Lisbon, yeah?' the man replied in a strong north-east Brazilian accent, which confirmed her initial thoughts.

Themis examined the Portuguese national identity card he presented her with. As soon as she took it from him, she felt that there was something not quite right about it. It was heavier than it should have been. She checked it under a UV light and noticed signs that suggested the presence of glue. When any type of adhesive is used on travel documents – for example, when the holder's photo is replaced with a different one – it makes the affected area stand out in a contrasting colour when it is exposed to UV light.

'So, where were you born?'

'In Lisbon'. He pronounced the word unlike any Portuguese person she had ever heard.

'Could you sing the Portuguese national anthem for me, please?' Themis asked him without warning.

'It's... erm...'.

'OK, second chance. What colour is the Portuguese flag?'

'But... it's... what do you mean?'

Good grief, he hasn't even bothered to learn the most basic stuff or thought about what he was going to say to us.

Not that this would have made any difference. It had been naive at best of him to think he could get through one of the busiest airports in the world, full of the most experienced officers in the business, with a forged Portuguese ID card. Around eighty million passengers come through those gates every year, ninety four percent of them on international flights. It would be pretty much impossible to find a document that immigration officers had never seen before.

'Alright, let's get to the point. Where did you buy this document?'

'I didn't buy it. This is my own ID card'.

'Balder, can you get hold of a forgery officer so they can take a look at this document for me, please?' asked Themis.

She filled in an IS81 form and handed it to the passenger before taking him straight to the pan.

'So, you've identified your first forgery, Themis', said Balder. 'I'm proud of you. How did you work out that it was a fake?'

'I knew there was something wrong about that passenger even before he got to my desk. He stuck out like a sore thumb. You know that scene in Terminator, where Arnie looks at the guy's clothes and works out whether they'll fit him? He sort of scans each part of his body and the result comes out positive, you remember? That's what it was like. It was like the time you saw that guy filling in his landing card'.

'Exactly, Themis!' agreed Balder. 'It's often like that – nothing obvious. You just have that feeling that something isn't right, even without knowing exactly what it is. It can be something that they say, the way they're dressed, the way they talk to the officers, their body language... There are so many signs. A businessman wears a suit and tie like a second skin, he's so used to dressing like that. It's second nature to him. We have students coming in from all over the world, but the way some of them are dressed just doesn't sit properly with their reasons for being here... They'll turn up in a suit with dress shoes and no socks, carrying a really flashy James Bond-style briefcase. That lot go straight to the pan, no questions asked!'

'Don't you talk to them first?' asked Themis.

'Waste of time. They'll show you an acceptance letter, saying they're here to study for a Master's in Robotics, but they don't speak a word of English. All they can say is "yes sir", "yes ma'am"', replied Balder, imitating the passengers' accents.

'Well, at least I'll be able to get myself back in the boss' good books, considering things didn't start out so well this morning', said Themis.

They informed the chief immigration officer in the watch house of the case and added the passenger's details to the log of people under investigation. Themis and Balder then led him to the baggage area.

'How many bags did you bring?'

'Just one'.

Opening up his case, they saw that the young man had brought hardly any clothes with him; there were just enough for a few days. Themis took everything out and made a detailed analysis of the contents. She found a small pocket, almost hidden, at the bottom of the case. Inside this pocket, they found a passport.

Severino Auxêncio – Place of birth: Lagoa Grande – Pernambuco, Brazil.

'OK sir, so you weren't actually born in Lisbon, were you?'

'No, ma'am'.

'Balder, this gentleman told me in the initial desk interview that he had been born in Portugal, but it turns out that he was actually born in Brazil'.

'Have you been to the United Kingdom before?'

'No, this is my first time in Europe'.

Themis looked through his wallet. A quick inspection revealed two twenty-pound notes, an Oyster card for use on the London transport system, and a bank card issued in the United Kingdom three years earlier.

'Whose is this Oyster card?' she asked. 'If you've never been here before, where did this come from? And how did you manage to open a bank account? You've got a lot of explaining to do, Mr Auxêncio'.

This exchange reminded her of an incident in the control room of the supermarket where Themis used to work. It had been her second job in the United Kingdom, after she had left the fast-food place in the shopping centre. She needed to work had noticed that a supermarket near her home was advertising for check-out workers. She applied for one of the vacancies, and soon afterwards, she started working there. It was not particularly taxing and gave her the opportunity to use English every day. This was important for Themis, as she was convinced that she really needed to improve her English language skills. She had set this target for herself, she needed to speak English just as well as a British person in order to apply for jobs involving a greater degree of responsibility. From the day she arrived in the United Kingdom, she had no difficulty whatsoever understanding the BBC news on the television. However, feeling particularly adventurous one day, she had turned on the Graham Norton show and his Irish accent made things far more complicated. She could not understand a word of what he said, and his jokes went straight over her head!

Still, she always knew what was on special offer and could save money by buying discounted products that were reaching their sell-by date. Also, as an employee, she had a discount card, which made life a bit easier.

It's true, every little helps, she would tell herself.

It was just a normal day at work, and Themis was serving a very nice elderly lady. She had seen her shopping there before, but this was the first time she had come to Themis' till.

'Hello dear, how are you today?' asked the lady.

'I'm very well, thanks. And you? Do you need any help packing your things?'

'Yes, please. Thank you, that's most kind', replied the lady. 'By the way, have you tried these strawberry-and-cream sweets?' she asked Themis.

'Not yet, no', replied Themis, scanning the lady's shopping. Her trolley was full of sweet treats. *She certainly loves her sweet stuff*, thought Themis. *Maybe she shouldn't be eating so much sugar at her age. But she looks happy, and that's the main thing.*

'Here, try one. You won't regret it'.

'Oh, thanks, but you don't need to. I'll buy myself a packet later to try'.

'No, go on, you really have to try one', insisted the lady.

'OK'. Themis popped the sweet into her mouth and threw the wrapper into the waste basket under her till.

'Mmm, you weren't wrong! These are delicious. I'm definitely going to buy some for myself!'

As the lady finished paying for her groceries, another customer had already begun placing her things on the conveyor belt. Themis did not want to lose the sweet wrapper and quickly bent down to take it out of the waste bin, placing it in the transparent plastic folder where she kept the codes for products, such as fruit and vegetables that needed to be weighed at the till. She did all this as quickly as she could, so the next customer's shopping did not pile up on the conveyer belt. Sitting back in her chair, she started passing the products over the scanner. When she had almost finished, she saw her manager standing by the till. Themis then noticed that the manager had placed the 'Closed' sign on her till belt.

'When you're finished with this customer, please come and talk to me', said her manager.

'OK', replied Themis, finding this a little odd.

Themis closed her counter. She was working on till number thirteen – something she would never forget. *Lucky number,* she thought. She then walked towards the supervisor, who was waiting for her.

'Everything OK, Themis? We just need to clear up a couple of things with you. Can you come with me to the meeting room at the end of the corridor please?'

I knew I'd get in trouble for accepting that sweet, she thought. Together, they walked towards a small room. Themis only realised that this was the CCTV room once the supervisor opened the door and revealed a panel of screens, one for each of the cameras installed to watch over the supermarket, including one that was placed over the tills. In the room were Themis' supervisor and her manager, the security supervisor, and the general manager of the branch. Themis thought that it must be some sort of a training session.

'Themis, I'm going to show you something that we caught on the security cameras a short while ago, and then I'd like you to explain exactly what happened'.

I bet they've zoomed in on my mouth, with me sucking on the sweet and talking to a customer with my mouth full, she guessed. The video started with Themis bending down, as if to pick something up from under the till, and quickly placing an item – which appeared to be a pinkish red-coloured piece of paper – into her plastic folder.

'Can you explain what happened there, please?'

For a few seconds, she did not quite understand what was going on. They were clearly accusing her of taking something that did not belong to her. Possibly money. It suddenly occurred to her that a fifty-pound note was coloured the same shades of red and pink. *Do they really think I stole money from the till?*

Not for the first time, Themis felt the weight of prejudice weigh her down. Was this happening because she was an immigrant? Was it because of her accent? Or just the fact that she was a lowly check-out girl? Maybe all three? She felt humiliated, worth-less. Back in Brazil, she had been a quality control manager at the state telecommunications company. She held a degree from a good university. Themis wondered whether it had been worth putting herself through all this, moving away from her family and the friends she cherished so much. She also knew that her reasons for being here, so far away from everything that she held dear, had nothing to do with the economic situation in her country. The truth was that Themis had had her heart broken, and Brazil was no longer big enough to bear the pain that this, and a life plan thrown out of the window, had caused her. She needed to be far away, forget the past, erase it completely. In order to do this, she had put an ocean between herself and her country. Forever.

'Do you think I took money from the till?' she asked.

They looked at each other, and before anyone could say anything, Themis spoke:

'Well, I'm sorry to disappoint you, but what I took out of the waste bin was actually just a sweet wrap-per. A customer very kindly gave me a sweet while I was helping her with her shopping. I didn't want to lose the wrapper and there was a new customer at the till, so I had to be quick and not leave her wait-ing. Look'.

Themis opened her plastic folder and showed them the wrapper. She had never felt so humiliated in her entire life, but she realised that the situation could have been a whole lot worse. She thought about how it could have been had she not spoken English. *They would have crucified me,* she thought. They would have definitely called the police, and before she was able to explain, she would have been taken to the police station. Themis thought about how many immigrants had been through similar situations, having a voice but not being able to use it to defend themselves due to the language barrier.

'No one is accusing you, Themis. We just want you to explain what happened', said the head of security.

'I suppose if you *were* accusing me, the police would have been invited to this little meeting too, right? Well, I've explained what happened, and as everyone is here, I'll take this opportunity to let you all know that today will be my last day here'.

'Themis, you don't need to do that', said her manager.

'Yes, I do, and I'm doing it. I don't want to work at a place where I'm not trusted. I'll empty my locker and return my keys and uniform'.

'You'll need to work your notice', the store manager informed her.

Themis wanted to tell her where she could stick her notice, but she bit her lip and told her that they could take her to court if they were that bothered about it. She left the meeting room, unwilling to listen to anything else they had to say to her. She just wanted to get out of there and go somewhere she could cry without being seen. Somewhere she could let the tears run freely and hide her shame. In her heart, she knew that she was worth more than this, that one day she would go far, but these obstacles were difficult to overcome on her own, in the Land of Hope and Glory. Themis felt fragile and could still hear her father's words to her as she left Brazil: 'You won't last beyond the first winter in Europe'. She had to get through this; there was no other option for her. She composed herself, handed in her locker key, her badge, her discount card, and her uniform, and never set foot in the place again.

Severino's case was different. Themis had known that she was innocent and he clearly was not, but she still wanted to ensure that the procedure was carried out correctly and that the young man was treated as kindly and humanely as possible, without prejudice and in a dignified manner. In her heart, she felt sorry for him.

After checking his bags, Themis and Balder led Severino into the holding room, where the assistant officers took his photo and fingerprints. Once the passenger file was ready and the chief immigration officer had been updated on events, they began the formal interview.

'Is this your first time in the United Kingdom?'

'No, the truth is that I lived here for four years, but I had to go back home because my mum was ill'.

'How long did you stay in your country of origin?' asked Themis.

'I ended up staying for six months. While I was there, I met someone, and she got pregnant'.

'So, why didn't you stay in your country with your girlfriend?'

'Because we couldn't afford to pay for a house and the baby was about to be born. The plan was that she would follow me over here later'.

'Whose idea was it to get hold of fake papers?'

'I met a guy who said he could sort me out with the papers. I don't know his real name. He's known to be a bit dodgy. You know, I sold everything I owned to get here'.

'Mr Auxêncio, using forged documents is a crime in the United Kingdom. You can go to prison for it. Our superior will make the decision regarding whether you're going to be arrested and sent to court or if you'll just be refused entry and sent back to Brazil.

'Themis, in most cases, the State chooses just to send them back. It's a lot cheaper for the British taxpayer than to keep them all in prison. All we do is refuse these idiots entry, and then the airline has the dubious pleasure of their company for the next eleven hours', explained Balder.

'Mr Auxêncio, what were you doing during the four years you spent here?'

'I did what everyone does, ma'am. Worked on building sites and sent money home, to my mum', said the young man, showing no signs of remorse.

'And how come you didn't use your own passport?'

'I was stopped by immigration when I left the United Kingdom, when I was going back to Brazil. They took my fingerprints. I wouldn't have been able to get back here on my real passport'.

'OK, Mr Auxêncio. We're going to pass on all the information to our superior officer and be in touch with you as soon as we have a decision'.

Themis and Balder gave their recommendations to the chief immigration officer, who agreed that this passenger should be refused entry. Then, they called the airline to reserve his seat back to Brazil. To their surprise, the flight scheduled for that evening had been cancelled for technical reasons.

'Themis, we'll need to call the detention centre at Colnbrook to find out if they've got a bed for our guy.

He'll have to spend the night there before he flies back tomorrow'.

'OK, I'll do that now', said Themis.

'Right, Balder, it's all arranged', Themis informed Balder a while later. 'I've already sorted the escorts to take him to the detention centre, and his seat has been booked on tomorrow's flight. The escorts bringing him back to the airport have been booked as well. Boss and passenger have both been informed. Is there anything else we need to do?'

'Yes! Lunch! We worked the whole shift without a break! My treat, Themis', said Balder. 'Come to the duty-free area with me. I'm going to introduce you to the best croissant in the world!'

Balder knew the airport like the back of his hand: He could tell you where to go for the best coffee, the best bargains, the best place for a perfect view of the runway, and, of course, the best croissant in the world. Themis had never heard of such a thing as a croissant with cheese and ham, and it would have probably been better for her to never have found out. This guilty pleasure would become part of her routine, especially on days like this, which were particularly stressful.

Another working day had come to an end. Themis felt that she had fulfilled her duty. This evening, the passenger she had intercepted would tread upon

British soil for one last time, on his way to the detention centre. So close and yet so far from his dream, like the rain from his native city of Lagoa Grande, in the scorching hinterland of north-eastern Brazil.

CHAPTER 4

The Exceptional Medical Student

I need to fill up the car before I get onto the motorway, thought Themis. The needle on her fuel gauge had already dropped into the red.

Themis lived in Kent – an area known as 'the Garden of England'. It was famous for its beautiful green fields and for Bluewater – the third-biggest shopping centre in the United Kingdom. Every now and then, she would walk around the streets close to her home, although many of them had been built on steep slopes, which made the walk less enjoyable than it could have been. She would love to have had more time to really get to know the area, but the heavy traffic she encountered while driving to the other side of London at certain times of the day meant that she sometimes had to leave the house three hours before her shift began. As a result, she often chose to work the 'anti-social' shifts: the early one, which started at six in the morning and ended at quarter past one in the afternoon, or the last one of the day, from a quarter to four in the afternoon until eleven o'clock at night. She was driving up one of the steeply inclined roads that led to the closest petrol station to her when suddenly the car lost all power and the control panel went blank.

No! What's happening? This car is new, and there's still some fuel left in the tank! Come on, come on, just a bit further...

Themis could see the petrol station at the top of the hill, but the car was getting slower and slower. She had just enough time to swerve the car into the left-hand lane before it came to a total halt. There were no lay-bys on that stretch of road. She tried to restart the car a few times, but it was not cooperating. Finally, she got out of the car and, sitting on the grass by the side of the road, began to search her phone for the number of the emergency breakdown company. On the other side of the road, moving in the opposite direction, a police car was driving down the hill.

Hmm, well, they're not going to waste their precious time on me, she thought, going back to her phone.

When she looked up again, she saw that the police car was approaching her.

'Hello ma'am, can we help you?' asked the police officer, getting out of his car and looking at her uniform.

The police uniform was similar to hers, with the exception of the police hat with its distinctive black-and-white checked band, which was not worn by immigration officers.

'I think my car's run out of petrol. I was really tired after my shift yesterday and went straight home without filling it up', explained Themis.

'Let's have a look. Can I have the key?' he asked, as a second policeman got out of the car.

I bet it will start the first time when he tries. Argh! They're going to think that I'm a stupid woman who can't even start a car! Themis thought, anticipating their reaction.

People were walking by, and some stopped to watch. Cars tooted their horns, and the passengers inside waved.

'Looks like we've got it started, ma'am!' said the policeman, grinning at Themis. 'Don't worry, we'll follow behind to make sure you get to the petrol station, OK?'

'OK, thank you', said Themis, thinking *Why do these things always happen to me?*

Themis got into her car and started driving up the hill, towards the petrol station. She drove very slowly, touching the accelerator as lightly as she could in order to use as little fuel as possible. She looked in the rear-view mirror and saw the police car with its blue lights flashing but no siren. She could see that the two men were laughing heartily at her predicament.

Bloody idiots, she thought as she forced a smile onto her face. She pulled into the petrol station, and the police car followed her in and parked right behind her. The lights were still flashing.

They're probably making sure I'm OK, Themis thought. *Either that, or they don't think they've embarrassed me enough yet!*

'I think you'll be OK from here, madam, but if you ever require a personal escort in future, just give us a call and we'll come as quickly as we can', said one of the policemen. A smile played on his lips as he handed her a piece of paper with his phone number written on it.

'Of course, no problem, thank you'.

Themis put the piece of paper in her trouser pocket and filled her car. She could feel the curious gaze of the other drivers, the people inside the small convenience store, and a few nosy parkers who had stopped their cars to see what was going on.

Stupid busybodies! Have they got nothing better to do than gawk at me? She paid for her fuel and set off towards the airport. After today, she promised herself, she would always keep the tank full. As she drove, she thought about the good-looking policeman who had given her his mobile number.

Now that would be an interesting relationship, she thought. They would probably manage to meet up about once a month when their days off coincided. At least they would not get bored and there would be no time for arguments.

Themis was feeling more confident at work now that her probationary period under Balder had ended, but she had to admit that she missed her impeccable supervisor. Sometimes, if they were on the same shift, they swapped stories, and she still asked him for his advice on occasion.

It was summer now, and there was no time for slacking off at work; the flights just kept coming in, one after another. Themis sat in the general control area, and although she did not find working with European travellers particularly interesting, she remembered that it had been there that she'd encountered her first forged document. She opened her position straight away. She had learnt from Balder that the worst thing possible was to have a reputation as a lazy officer.

'Passport, please. Where are you travelling from? Are you travelling alone? What is the purpose of your journey?' asked Themis.

The initial questions were always the same, and after a few more standard questions, it was anyone's guess as to how the interview would end. The passenger's responses would determine whether they were sent to the pan, allowed entry into the kingdom of pound sterling, red phone boxes, Big Ben and fish and chips, or, in the worst-case scenario, refused entry. Themis had never before understood how a meal could be so representative of a country. Of the exotic British cuisine she had come to know since she had moved here, her personal favourite was the Sunday roast or maybe the ubiquitous bacon sandwich, which she loved, although of course, it faced a fierce competition from the terminal's ham-and-cheese croissant...

'Brazil. I flew out of Porto Alegre, but I had stopovers in São Paulo and then Paris before arriving in London', the young man replied.

'And what have you come here to do?' asked Themis.

'Tourism. My uncle paid for the flight as a gift because I passed my university entrance exams to study medicine'.

'Really? Congratulations', she said.

Alarm bells went off in Themis' mind when the passenger said that he was going to study medicine. Medical students, who studied long and hard to compete for some of the most highly contested university places in the country, tended to speak particularly good English and were, as a general rule, very bright. This passenger had understood nothing of what Themis had asked him in English.

'So, what were your specialist subjects?' she asked.

Officers did not need to know the answers to all the questions they asked. The important thing was to note the way passengers reacted to these questions. If they answered quickly, without much of a delay, they were probably telling the truth. If they looked up at the ceiling to gain time or thought too hard about their responses, it was a sign that something was not quite right. Even those who were used to lying, the 'professional' liars, tended to slip up sooner or later. To be a good liar, one needed an excellent memory. One of Themis' favourite TV personalities was Judge Judy, whose catchphrases included the excellent motto, 'If it doesn't make sense, it's probably not true!'

'Eh? Spec... what?'

'Specialist', she repeated.

There was a long pause.

'I don't know what that is. I just sat the exam, and I passed', replied the passenger after some hesitation.

'When you sit for university entrance exams, specialist subjects cover the most important elements of the course you're trying to get into. And the tests for these subjects are in the form of essays. In your chosen career, the specialist subjects would probably have been physics, biology and chemistry', Themis patiently explained. 'Which university did you apply to?' she then asked.

'Federal University of Rio Grande do Sul'.

'OK, this is form IS81. It explains why we've

stopped you and the powers that we have to do so. I'm going to do some checks and will be back with you soon'.

'OK', replied the passenger.

Themis went to the watch house, where she noted down his details in the logbook and gave the chief immigration officer a summary of what had happened thus far. Once he gave her authorisation to carry out further checks, she went to the back office and logged on to the first available computer. She went online and found the public notice listing the names of students who had passed the entrance exam to study medicine at the university named by the passenger. She printed off all the available lists and searched carefully for his name. Unsurprisingly, she could not find it on there.

Not only has he lied, but he chose one of the most difficult universities to get into to back up his lie! It's just as I thought. He didn't pass any entrance exam!

Themis remembered Balder's words on her first day at the airport: 'They are all liars until they can prove they're not!'

'Pedro Henrique, this is the list of people who passed the entrance exam to study medicine. I can't see your name on here. So, I wondered if you could find it for me?'

'Hmm, I don't know why my name isn't on the list', said the young man, without bothering to try and find it or even pretending to look.

Themis liked to give the passengers she encountered plenty of rope. Although, by this time, she had already worked out that he was lying, she wanted to see just how far he was prepared to go. She did not know if he just wanted to make her believe that he had a promising career in his home country or if he was using the lie in an attempt to get into the country for some other reason. For most people, this was usually to find work. Or someone to have a 'relationship' with. Or both. It may be that it had always been his dream to become a doctor – something that he had never managed to achieve in his native land – and that, in his imagination, he was still living that life. He had perhaps carefully planned the story that he had told her – or maybe he had just said whatever came into his head at the time.

'Come with me please. We're going to have a look at your bags', she said.

In the baggage hall, Pedro Henrique looked nervous. He bit his nails and pulled up his trousers every five minutes. *Maybe he needs a cigarette,* thought Themis.

'How many bags did you bring?' she asked.

'Just the one'.

Themis opened the case and started to pull out some clothes, then two pairs of shoes, personal hygiene products and, finally, a brown envelope that aroused her suspicions, as it was stashed right at the bottom of the case, almost hidden away.

'What's in this envelope?' she asked.

'Just photos and some papers'.

Themis opened the envelope and looked carefully at each item as she took it out. Inside, there was a photo of a young woman, another photo of an older lady, a greetings card in the shape of a heart, and a letter.

'All documents of interest will be confiscated. Don't worry, they'll all be given back to you when we're done', she informed him.

'But those are personal. I don't want you to read them', he protested.

'That form I gave you after the initial interview explains that we have the power to seize any document or item belonging to passengers under investigation. Everything that is discussed between us is confidential. We won't keep your documents. As I already told you, you'll be given everything back when we've done. You'll have the opportunity to explain, in detail, the purpose of your visit to the United Kingdom. We know that you haven't come here as a tourist. Am I wrong?'

The passenger did not even bother to reply. He knew that his lie was about to be discovered, and he needed to come up with some other convincing story. He became serious, and it appeared as though his mind was far away.

Themis had always believed that the hard work she had put in over the years would be rewarded one day. Her first job with the British civil service had been at what was then known as the Inland Revenue, now Her Majesty's Revenue and Customs (HMRC). She had met her first mentor, Michael, there. Her mind flashed back to position number thirteen, the till she had occupied in her previous job at the supermarket, and she thought about how that number had, after all, turned out to be a lucky one for her. It was not long after the control room incident, when she had been accused of stealing, that she decided to move to Kent and applied for a job in the British civil service.

There had been every reason for her not to be successful in her application, but, as she used to tell herself, *When something is written in the stars, there's not much you can do about it.*

Themis found out about the vacancies on the last day of the application period, from a free local newspaper that was posted through her letterbox one morning. She called her nearest Inland Revenue office to ask for an application form, not knowing then that she would be working in that same office in the near future. The receptionist confirmed what Themis already knew:

'Today is the last day to apply, madam, but you could come and pick one up in person if you wish'.

Themis quickly left her house and arrived at the reception area at around half past two that afternoon.

'What time do you close, please?'

'At five p.m.', replied the receptionist, the same one Themis had spoken to on the phone earlier that day.

'Have you got a free room available where I could fill in my form?' asked Themis. 'I'm really interested in applying for one of these vacancies'.

'Yes, come with me. There's an interview room on this floor. It isn't going to be used for the rest of the day'.

At one of her first personal development meetings, Michael created a detailed profile for Themis. He asked her where she saw herself working in the future, about her ambitions, her qualifications, and her previous work experience. She replied that her dream was to work for the Home Office one day.

'Themis, why the Home Office? What makes you want to work for the immigration service?' he had asked.

'I like dealing with the public, and I have a lot of experience in customer service. Also, I think that speaking another language will give me a bit of an edge, something that'll be useful for working at the airport'.

'And you think that you will work for immigration one day?' he asked, showing interest in the new recruit.

'I think that we always have opportunities to chase our dreams. We just have to keep working towards them, don't we?'

'You're absolutely right, Themis', Michael had agreed.

One morning, exactly two years after that meeting, Michael waited anxiously for Themis to arrive at the office. When she got there, he ran to tell her that the time had come: The Home Office was recruiting.

'Really, Michael?' asked Themis. She was not especially excited, although it had come as a surprise.

By then, she was working as an executive secretary in the department. She was comfortable in the job, and the fact that she could cycle to work made it even better. The department had paid for the bicycle and all the equipment, including a lock and a helmet. This was part of a green initiative programme – where the government provided employees with loans to buy non-polluting forms of transport and the employees then paid back the loan in small installments. This meant one less car on the roads and the satisfaction of doing the right thing for the environment. Furthermore, it helped Themis keep in shape and improved her quality of life.

However, it had not been easy in the beginning. She was being trained to replace a woman who was about to retire. Themis had had to put up with the frustrated ambitions of this woman, who would rather have been training her own daughter to take over. Unfortunately, she had not got through the application stage, which would have enabled her to get an interview and, if successful, take on the position. The woman did not even try to hide her initial adverse feelings from Themis, although she had slowly come to realise that it was not the fault of her young replacement.

It was a small department, consisting of two typists, the woman who was about to retire, the head of department, and now Themis. In the two years she had worked there, she felt as though she was a part of a small family. The typists, both middle-aged, would gently make fun of Themis, without malice though – at least, it did not seem to Themis that there was anything unkind in the way they teased her. She had been in the United Kingdom for less than three years, and her Brazilian accent was still quite strong, leading her to pronounce vowel sounds at the ends of words, where they did not belong. She noticed that the two ladies giggled whenever she talked about the Spice Girls, but she never understood why that was. Time passed, and one day, around Easter, they were having a small party in the office. The subject of the Spice Girls came up:

'Themis, what's the name of that girl band you like so much?'

'What, the *Spicy* Girls?'

They laughed again.

'Why do you find it so funny when I talk about the *Spicy* Girls?' asked Themis.

'We think it's cute, Themis. Say it again. Can you not hear the difference between the words "spice" and "spicy"?' they asked her.

Themis went as red as a lobster when she realised the mistake she had been making all this time. Everyone in the room found this hilarious, even the grumpy manager who was hardly ever there.

'Michael, thanks for remembering about the Home Office. I wasn't even thinking about that anymore', said Themis.

'Ah, well, I never forgot, you see. You remember when we did your professional profile a couple of years ago?' he asked.

'I do, yes'.

'Well, I'm not going to let you just sit back in your comfort zone. One of my jobs is to look after your personal development. Let's finish filling in the form. I've already taken care of your references', said Michael.

What's this form he's on about? thought Themis. Her comfort zone felt like a rather good place to be in at that moment.

'What form, Michael?' she finally asked, taking off her helmet.

She was not sure if he was really thinking about her personal development or if he just wanted to get her out of the way as he could not deal with being around her anymore. Themis knew Michael was attracted to her, even though he tried to hide it. He was always there, ready to help her. He was like her guardian angel in human form. Before she even realised that she needed help, he was there. It was almost as though there was some form of intuition that alerted him when she was having difficulties. Maybe having her in the department was causing him too much of a personal conflict; after all, he was a married man. So, he was prepared to help his muse progress professionally, even if – or maybe because - hcr succcss would put a physical distance between them.

'The form to apply for a position as a visa officer. Your dream of working for the British immigration service is about to come true, Themis. Aren't you excited?' he asked.

'Yes, of course', she replied, not wanting to disappoint him. She wondered why Michael was so certain she would get the job

Three months later, Themis was saying farewell to the department. They had a whip-round for her, raising £100, and organised a leaving party. She only found out on her last day that Michael was on leave, and she never got to thank him for everything he had done for her. She thought about him every time she got another promotion in the following years and sent him an email, letting him know the news. Michael never replied. Many times, she thought about calling him but decided to respect his decision to cut ties in the end.

The phoney medical student's file was ready, and Themis started checking the items she had found in his suitcase. The letter she had found inside the brown envelope contained a lot more than just personal information. It told Themis everything she needed to know about the young man's journey to London:

'My darling son, I'm going to miss you so much, but I know that you're chasing your dreams, and this

gives my heart some comfort. I pray to God that you'll find work quickly and that all your dreams come true. The only thing I ask is that you never forget your mum. I love you. God bless you. Call me as soon as you can'.

On the back of one of the photos, there was the following message: *'I love you very much. Come back soon, Helena'.* The photo of Helena was inside a heart-shaped greetings card, containing declarations of love that could only have been made by someone whose heart ached at the thought of not seeing the person they loved for a very long time. Themis was getting better at her job. This guy had tried to lie his way past her, but he did not stand a chance of getting into the United Kingdom with so much evidence against him. She knew how frustrated he would be and how this would affect his life. He had left everything he knew behind: his mother, his girlfriend, his dream of becoming a doctor, and the cold nights drinking *mate* – a traditional tea-like beverage of his region – with friends, next to the burning fire outside his house. Themis' English friends were often surprised to hear that Brazil was not all sunshine, rainforest, and beach volleyball. In the southernmost region of the country, where Pedro Henrique came from, it was mountainous and often bitterly cold. His motivation was the same as many who had come before him: to achieve a better life, no matter how far it had to be from everything that made him happy.

Themis believed that when ordinary people lied – as opposed to compulsive liars – they did it because they found themselves backed into a corner. And although those lies often left her feeling disappointed in her fellow humans, she understood that, in most cases, people would try absolutely anything to get an opportunity to change their lives, even if they ran the risk of leaving themselves exposed and defenceless in the process. There was no acceptable justification for lying. Yes, she understood why people did it, but, at the end of the day, she had a job to do.

'Are you feeling OK, Pedro Henrique?' Themis asked at the start of the interview.

'I'm feeling a bit confused…', he replied.

'Why? Did you think it would be easier to get into the United Kingdom?' she asked.

'I just don't know why you decided to pick on me'.

'I'm an immigration officer. It's my job to *scrutinise* passengers. Not just you, but any passenger who tries to pull the wool over my eyes. Now, I must remind you that this is a formal interview. My questions and your responses will all be noted down in your file. At the end, this record of interview will be read by a chief immigration officer, who will decide whether you should be allowed into the United Kingdom or refused entry. I should also remind you that it's a crime to lie to an immigration officer and that if we discover that you're lying to us, you will be refused entry and banned from entering the United Kingdom for ten years. Did you understand all of that?'

'Yes'.

'So, what is the reason for your visit to the United Kingdom?'

'I'm here as a tourist'.

'I found a letter from your mother in your suitcase. She said that she hoped you found a job quickly', said Themis, taking the letter out of the folder. 'What can you tell me about that?'

'It's true. I've come for a holiday, but if a job opportunity comes up, I'll take it'.

'And don't you know that it's illegal to work without a work visa? You're asking me for permission to come into the country as a tourist!'

'Yeah, but that's what everyone does. They come to earn money. I spent three thousand *reais* to get here. I want to earn that back at least'.

'Unfortunately, that's not going to be possible, Pedro Henrique. The purpose of a tourist visa is to allow people to come and visit the country, and they return to their countries of origin at the end of the visit. It's not supposed to be an easy form of entry for people who want to get around the system. My job is to stop that from happening'.

Themis went on:

'I'm going to recommend to my superior that you be refused entry on this occasion. If your personal circumstances change in the future and you wish to return to the United Kingdom, my advice is that you apply for a tourist visa before travelling. Here is the envelope that I seized earlier. You will return to your country on the next available flight. Immigration is obliged to send you back to the first point of your national territory, even if this is not where you started your journey'.

'Can't you send me to Paris?' he asked.

'I'm afraid not. We can only send people to countries where we're certain they will be accepted. You don't have residence in Paris, so we have to send you back to your country of origin'.

'Where can I get advice on my rights?'

'Passengers who try to enter a country by deception don't really have many rights. If you're referring to your human rights, you're free to exercise them in your own country. You don't have any links with this country; you don't have family here and you have never set foot outside Brazil before. Is there anything else I can help you with?'

'No. I'm never coming back to this place again'.

'That, of course, is your choice. If you've understood everything, please sign here. Have a great journey back. If you want anything to eat, just ask the guards. There's a payphone in the detention area. If you want me to give the number to a family member, just let me know'.

'Thanks', said Pedro Henrique, not sounding very thankful.

At the exit to the holding room, one of the guards asked Themis if she was sending that passenger home as well. Her fame for refusing entry to all and sundry was well established. She nodded. She felt no pleasure at having the second highest number of refusals under her belt – second only to Balder, of course. It was obvious that an officer working with flights coming from certain areas with high incidences of refusals, if they were doing their job properly, would also have the highest number of refusals. Coincidence or not, the department had a certain preference for having her work on the shift starting at a quarter to two. This was just around the time at which the flight from Brazil arrived at the terminal.

Relieved to have finished work for the day, Themis decided to stop for a coffee. She needed to wake up a bit before hitting the motorway. *Funny how adrena-*

line stops as soon as we leave the terminal and take off our uniform insignia, thought Themis. *It's like we cast off our superpowers and become human again. Great power brings great responsibility.* Her actions had, once again, changed the course of someone's life and, although she had done the right thing, this would leave another set of fingerprints on her soul.

She parked the car in front of her house – a miracle in itself, as this was something that she was rarely able to do at that time of the night. As she went to open the door, she was surprised to see a red rose tied to the doorknob. There was also a message, which read, 'It was very nice to meet you. Matt'.

Themis went into the house, threw her uniform into the washing machine, took a shower, and went to bed. She placed the rose on her bedside table before she fell asleep.

CHAPTER 5

Russian Roulette

Shit! Shit!

Themis jumped out of bed and ran towards the washing machine. According to the living room clock, it was exactly 2:22 a.m.

Oh no, my uniform trousers are covered in bits of paper!

The phone number of the handsome police officer, called Matt, as Themis had learnt the night before, was now a soggy clump of paper! In her haste to get everything done before she went to bed the previous night, she had thrown her uniform into the washing machine, forgetting that the piece of paper with his number on it was still in the pocket of her trousers.

Now I won't be able to thank him for the rose. He's going to think I'm so rude, she thought.

Unsuccessfully, Themis tried to get back to sleep. She had realised by now that shift work affected her physically, as it would any mere mortal. This was why the British government paid good money, with several additional perks, for the privilege of having highly specialised workers at its service twenty-four hours a day. It had to be this way, unfortunately. Passengers would sometimes arrive at half-past four in the morning, and flights did not stop arriving until very late at night. If flights were delayed, it could be as late as one in the morning when they arrived. Then, if a passenger was stopped, they had to be interviewed, and this could take immigration officers into the early hours of the morning and beyond. Studies showed that people working under these conditions tended to develop a series of health problems and ended up with a lower life expectancy than those who never had to work shifts.

Themis arrived at the airport and, as always, stopped at the Italian café in the arrivals lounge, next to the security area used by airport staff. The man working behind the counter knew that Themis always had an Americano with a cheese-and-ham panini. Sometimes, she would treat herself to a mini chocolate panettone to eat later, if she had the time, or on her way home. She liked the idea of being able to eat panettone all year round and not just at Christmas.

A short while later, Themis was sitting at her post in the arrivals hall, having just opened up her counter. She was preparing herself for another day of action when she heard a woman's voice shouting at her daughter not to run. The immigration control was practically empty, and Themis saw a little girl with golden curls running towards her desk, carrying a teddy bear that was nearly as big as the child herself.

'Hey, where d'you think you're off to, young lady? You can't get through here without showing me your passport – and his passport as well!' Themis squatted down, blocking the exit and pointing to the little girl's bear.

The passengers in the queue started laughing.

'No problem, miss', replied the little girl.

The girl's mother finally caught up with her. She was holding three passports: her own, the little girl's, and another one that belonged to the bear.

'Your bear has a passport?' asked Themis, somewhat taken aback.

'He has, and it's got loads of stamps in it', replied the little girl with pride, holding onto her teddy bear.

Themis looked at the passport and was surprised to see just how many countries the bear had been to. She was in no doubt that she was dealing with a genuine visitor here. It had an enviable collection of stamps – far more well-travelled than some of the fake tourists who had come to her desk in recent times! Themis stamped the three passports, handing back the one belonging to the bear to the little girl.

'Thank you! He didn't have one of these yet'. The girl smiled at Themis and gave her hand to her mum, who was now holding the teddy bear.

'Passport, please', she called to the next passenger in the queue.

A young man came to her desk and handed Themis his passport.

'Good morning, where have you travelled from today? Are you travelling alone?' she asked

'Brazil'.

'Where did you change flights?' asked Themis. 'There aren't any direct flights from Brazil at this time of the morning'.

'Does it matter?' the young man arrogantly asked.

'Er, it does actually, yes', Themis responded curtly.

Immigration officers paid remarkably close attention to passengers' prior movements. The countries they had entered and any stopovers they had made could be an indication of whether they were trafficking drugs or attempting to trick immigration into believing they were genuine tourists. Themis knew only too well that some passengers would do this by buying package tours that involved quick stopovers in several European countries. By doing this, they sought to create a false impression that they had enough money to do a grand tour of Europe; however, very often, these passengers were not in the least bit interested in seeing the countries they visited and would sleep in train stations or airports without even going to see the sights of whatever city they happened to be in at the time. All they were interested in was creating a travel history in their newly issued passports, filling the clean pages with stamps. It was not unheard of for officers to find a United

States visa in an otherwise empty passport but with no evidence of it having been used – it would just be there to fill a couple of pages. The fake tourist's reasoning was, 'If I'm good enough for the United States, then I'm good enough for the United Kingdom'.

The work of immigration control is extremely important. Immigration officers are very highly trained and become used to hearing the same stories time and again. They become specialists in human nature and can categorise the behaviour exhibited by *the pseudo passengerum* species by their place of birth and the passport they present. Looking on from a distance, even before checking a single passport, officers knew which flight had just arrived in the terminal, from the behaviour of the passengers as they come into the arrivals hall. Impeccably dressed men wearing sunglasses and speaking in loud voices? Easy, the Alitalia flight had just come in. Not to mention the absence of anything resembling order, as the concept of queuing was unheard of in Italy. Organised groups, with passengers all wearing the same T-shirt and following a leader holding up a board? That would be the flight from China. Young men with sun-kissed hair and skin, smelling of board wax and wearing brightly coloured clothes? Australian surfers arriving to brighten up the cold, grey streets of London!

The young man replied truculently, apparently unwilling to interact with her: 'Madrid'.

'What is the purpose of your visit to the United Kingdom?'

'Study and visit'.

'Where's the letter from the school?'

'Letter? What letter? I haven't got a letter. Listen, do you know who you're talking to? My father is a very high-ranking officer in the Brazilian police', said the young man in a menacing tone.

'I ask the questions here. Your job is to answer them. Who your father is and what he does for a living is not the issue here. Go and sit over there until I call you, OK?' said Themis, losing her patience with him. 'And I suggest you think hard about your attitude before I call you over again'.

Ugh, some people, she thought with a grimace. *You can take the boy out of Brazil, but it seems you can't take Brazil out of the boy.*

She left him stewing in the pan until all the other passengers had gone through immigration, then signalled for him to come to her desk.

'Good morning, where have you travelled from today? Are you travelling alone?' Themis asked for a second time.

'I've just arrived from Brazil, but I changed flights in Madrid. I'm here to do a short English course and some tourism'.

'How long are you intending to stay here? Please show me your return ticket and the letter from the school of English'.

'Here's my return ticket. I'm going back to Brazil on the 19th October, so I'll be here for just over three weeks. I'm afraid I didn't print out the letter from the school, but I have it on my mobile. Would you like to see it?'

'OK, I'm going to give you permission to enter for one month. This will be enough time for you to study and get to see a bit of the country. Everything we've discussed today will be recorded on the system. This means that you'll be questioned again when you enter the United Kingdom in the future. Consider yourself lucky. If you'd spoken like that to one of my colleagues', – Themis indicated the officers at the desks next to hers – 'you'd be on the next flight back to Brazil. And a word of advice: that sort of thing doesn't work here; no one here really cares who your father is. Enjoy your stay', said Themis, handing the passenger his documents back.

The young man scuttled away from Themis' desk as quickly as he could without saying anything else.

'Next. Passport, please', called Themis.

'Good morning', said a young couple as they approached her desk.

'Where have you come from today?'

'Saint Petersburg', said the woman.

'Have you come on business or for pleasure?'

'He's coming home because he lives here, and I'm here on holiday'.

'How do you know one another?', asked Themis.

'We're friends'.

As she replied to Themis' last question, the woman looked away. She ran her right hand over her hair, tucking a loose strand behind her ear. As she did this, Themis was momentarily dazzled by the glittering ring she was wearing. It was not just the beauty of the ring that struck Themis but also the fact that she would have liked to be in that position herself: married to the love of her life, building the home of her dreams. All she had ever wanted was true love, a child, and a place to live that she could call home. She noticed how brightly the stones in the ring shone and concluded that it was probably new.

If she's just got married, why isn't she on her honeymoon? And more to the point, why is she on a holiday with a friend and not her husband?

Themis reflected once more on the words of Judge Judy: 'If something doesn't make sense, it's probably not true'.

'Why didn't your husband come on holiday with you?' asked Themis.

'My husband is working at present'.

Newly married and travelling with another man... Does she think I was born yesterday?

Themis scanned the man's British passport and asked him to go through, explaining to the female passenger that she was going to have to make further enquiries regarding her visit.

'Mrs Sorokina, we need to ask you some more questions. Your friend can carry on with his journey and collect his bags'.

The man said goodbye and walked towards the escalator that led down to the baggage hall.

Themis passed on the details of the case to the chief immigration officer and then took the woman downstairs so she could take a look at her belongings.

'How long are you planning to spend here on holiday?'

'Just two weeks', replied the woman, looking a little nervous.

'How many suitcases did you bring?'

'Two'.

Themis took the woman's cases from the con-veyer belt; they were as heavy as lead. *I hope these aren't full of nail varnish,* she thought, remembering the episode with the elderly manicure lady. Many months had passed since that day. She was much more confident now and remembered that Balder had once told her that just a few questions were gen-erally enough to decide whether a passenger should be thrown into the pan or not. Themis had never imagined back then that she would one day be able to identify a suspicious passenger simply from the way she turned her face, or smoothed her hair, or by a ring she wore on the ring finger of her right hand. She knew that Russians wore their wedding rings on the right hand. This was something they had taken from the Romans, who considered the left hand un-lucky; it also indicated a lack of trust. The Christian Orthodox Church inherited this custom, which sub-sequently filtered down to the different populations that made up the country of Russia.

Nothing beats a bit of learning! Themis smiled to herself. She was now a fully paid-up 'immigration rat', as Balder used to call them. Good old Balder, he was always right. She missed him. She missed his grumpy moments as much as she did his kindness.

It's a shame he's already been snapped up, she thought. Maybe she was fated to always be on her own; she had even lost the number of the man who had been interested in her.

Themis started looking through the contents of the suitcase, making a mental note of things that were worthy of special attention: some very tasteful items of lingerie and *six* packs of contraceptive pills.

Back in the office, once she had completed her inspection, Themis prepared to formally interview the Russian woman. She created a record for her on the system, added some extra pages for the interview, and walked towards the detention room. She stopped in the staff changing rooms to leave her landing stamp safely in her locker. Ever since that time she had taken it home by accident, she was extra careful with it. It was probably a good thing that the incident had shaken her up so much, because it meant that she avoided getting herself into the sort of trouble that some of her colleagues had experienced. Time and time again, officers would leave their stamps on the control desk. They were all trained to take care of their own stamps and those of their colleagues. If any of them left their personal stamp on the desk, it would be the responsibility of the next colleague, who, in turn, was obliged to ensure its safety. This involved handing it in to the chief immigration officer, which generally meant trouble. Most of them would rather hide the stamp and let their colleagues sweat while they unsuccessfully searched for it. Themis remembered one officer who would attach one end of a metal chain to the stamp and have the other end connected to her waistband. She had been in trouble so many times for leaving it lying about that she could not risk it happening again. Even rigged up like this, she still managed to leave the stamp on the desk. On more than one occasion, Themis had seen her close her position and walk away with the stamp still hanging from her waistband on the chain, bumping against her backside as she walked.

She handed the Russian passenger's file to the assistant immigration officers, who would take her fingerprints and carry out all the safety checks. In the meantime, she decided to go and have something to eat in the staff canteen. When she got there, she was slightly annoyed to see that one of the few officers she did not really get on with was sitting in there. Themis called him 'subway ghost', after the character in 'Ghost' who told Patrick Swayze to get off the train and thought of himself as the boss of the metro. This particular officer thought he was the boss of the terminal.

'Hi Themis, how are you? What are you up to?' he asked.

'Not much', she replied, reluctant to get into a conversation with him.

'I was just thinking. You've not been living here for long, have you? You won't know much about our culture then. I'm surprised you managed to get this job. It's odd that you'd never have known about stuff like Queen, for example', he said.

'Well, for starters, the band was formed in 1970. I wasn't even born at that time! But I'm glad you brought them up though. You know Freddie Mercury was a foreigner, right? He was born in Tanzania, then grew up in India, before coming to England with his family. Did you know that? I'm so pleased that you recognise the contribution that foreigners like me have made to your country', said Themis, not even trying to hide the heavy sarcasm in her tone. 'Now, if you don't mind, I've got an interview to get to'.

It was not the first time that this officer had made barbed comments about her not being born in the United Kingdom. Themis never let comments like these get to her though, since she had got used to being on the receiving end of prejudice and negative reactions in the time she had been in this country. You had to stand up to that sort of thing, and it had felt good to put the "subway ghost" in his place. She left the kitchen and walked towards the holding room next door.

Like my dad used to say, if you can't say anything nice, don't say anything at all, thought Themis.

She signed the entry log and went into the room where the Russian woman was waiting.

'Hi, Mrs Sorokina, my name's Themis, and I need to ask you some questions about your arrival in the United Kingdom'.

Themis explained the procedure, and after reassuring herself that the woman felt well enough to be interviewed, she began.

'What is the purpose of your trip to the United Kingdom?'

'Tourism'.

'How long are you planning to stay here?'

'About two weeks', said the woman.

'When did you get married?'

'Three weeks ago. My husband had to stay behind for work'.

'Why didn't you wait until your husband got time off work to go on holiday?'

'It'll be ages before he gets any holiday time. He has a management job'.

'It just seems very odd to me that you would travel abroad with a friend after just getting married. Why do you need enough contraceptive pills for six months if you're only intending to stay here for two weeks?'

'Well, I like to be prepared', she said, trying to justify herself.

'Mrs Sorokina, your behaviour and the things I found in your suitcase lead me to believe that you will stay in the United Kingdom for more than two weeks. Your tourist visa ends at the end of this month, and yet you've got both summer and winter clothes in your case. This also suggests that you're not telling me the whole story. In addition to all this, you brought along six months' worth of contraceptives with you. Tell me what's really going on here?'

'OK, so the man I was traveling with is actually my husband. We decided to get married at the last minute and didn't want to be apart after the wedding'.

'Why didn't you apply for a spouse visa in Russia?' asked Themis.

'It takes twelve weeks for your government to deal with the application process. That's too long'.

'The British government offers a priority visa service. You could have gone for that option', said Themis.

'We were going to apply for the visa once we got here. I wouldn't stay here illegally'.

'The law requires that you apply for the visa in your country of residence – in your case, Russia. You can't come into the country as a visitor and then change it to a family visa, even though your husband has a British passport now'.

'But he has a friend who is also Russian born and his wife is French, and they did it'.

'The laws are different, Mrs Sorokina. You are Russian, and your husband is British. As I explained, British immigration law requires that you apply for a spouse visa while you are still in Russia. If your husband's friend's spouse is European – in this case, French – they would fall under a different set of regulations. European citizens are allowed to travel with their spouses and ask for a residence card here in the United Kingdom. There are some exceptions, but they don't relate to your case. Each case is different, and for you, the important thing is that you need to regularise your status back in your country of origin. I'm afraid I have to refuse you entry on this occasion. You asked for permission to enter the country as a tourist, whereas, in truth, you weren't coming here for a visit but to live with your husband. Your visa isn't valid for this purpose. I recommend that you apply for a spouse visa as soon as you get back to your country. Did you understand all of that?' asked Themis.

'Yes', sobbed the woman.

'I'll be back later to give you the details of your return flight. You can call your husband from the payphone in the waiting room. Don't worry, this is only temporary. You'll be able to come back to the United Kingdom as soon as you have the right visa'.

She was only doing her job, but Themis could never stop herself from imagining how she would feel if she were in the passenger's shoes. She felt bad for the people she stopped from coming into the country. In the Russian passenger's case, she knew it was only going to be temporary, and that if she followed the correct procedure, she would not have any problems. Despite the fact that Themis was working for the British government, she would always give advice if she was able to. As a general rule, she had a lot of patience, except in exceptional circumstances. Patience was very much a virtue in her line of work. The five years she had spent working at one of the biggest call centres in Brazil had taught her a great deal about the art of customer service. She had been employed to take calls from customers requesting connections and repairs to telephone lines and fielded the complaints that inevitably arose from people who were so dissatisfied with those services that they would call her department, breathing fire down the telephone. The main complaint Themis had to deal with was when the company did not respect its own deadlines. It would promise the customer that their phone line would be installed by a given date and then not do it. This meant that the customer stayed at home all day waiting for the line installer, who would then turn up at the customer's door and tell them that it was not possible to connect to the network serving that address. Sometimes, under great duress, they would install a line for a particularly threatening customer, but it meant having to disconnect someone else's in order to do so. Themis provided complainants with a blow-by-blow account: 'Telemar, Themis speaking, good morning, how may I help you?'

'Yes, I very much hope you can help. One of your people came to install my phone, and when he came down from the pole, I managed to catch him before he sneaked off. He said something about there not being any connection facility? I really can't believe it's so difficult to install a phone line! Please put me through to your supervisor!'

'Sir, I understand you're upset. When the installer goes to your home, he has to check the little box at the top of the pole. For your line to be connected, there needs to be some free wires available in the cable to pair it with…'.

'And you lot don't know if there are any free wires in the box before you send someone here and leave me sitting at home all day? Put me onto your supervisor!'

'I will, of course, but let me explain what the problem is first. When I'm done, if you still want to talk to my supervisor, I'll put the call through to him, is that OK?

'I know, I know. Every time I call you, I spend half an hour listening to that bloody annoying music and then you make an appointment and they either don't turn up or don't do anything when they get here!'

'Sir, as I was explaining, sometimes the line installer arrives on site and it isn't until they check the box on the telephone pole that they realise that these wires aren't available to pair up. Sometimes they're defective, but we can only test them at the time of installation. It's not the installer's fault. When this happens, we have to fix the network and install new cables, which takes time. Let me look at your record on our system. Just a moment please'.

'You're not going to make me listen to that music again, are you?' the customer said.

'No, sir... Oh, just a moment, the system is down... Can you confirm your phone number, please? What's your full name and address?' asked Themis. 'Ah, OK, it's back up again. Yes, you're right, it says here that your line wasn't installed at the new address, and as I explained, this was because there were no free wires available to pair it with. We call this the connection facility'.

'That's what the installer told me'.

'Yes, well, that's what it is. Oh, and I've got good news for you, sir. I have your new number here. Would you like to write it down?'

'Yes, of course. Thank God, I've got a number. That's great, thank you'.

'And I've got some more good news for you... you'll be receiving a digital line!'

'OK... and what are the advantages of having a digital line? I hope that doesn't mean you're putting the prices up?'

'No, sir. Your internet will be faster, and you'll also have access to special services such as call diversion and call waiting'.

'I don't care about special services. I just want my line installed!'

'Of course, but you just told me you missed a day's work. The call diversion service means that you'll be able to divert your landline calls to another number of your choice – even if you're in another part of the country. So, if you're waiting for an important call but need to leave the house, you won't risk missing it. You'll be able to receive it on your mobile phone, from wherever you happen to be. If you work for yourself, for example, and receive more than one call at the same time, you can put one person on hold while you talk to the other one. We've got a great promotion on at the moment. You can try out these services for one month, free of charge. How does that sound? I can add them to your package. You'll only be charged for them after the second month. If you don't find them useful, just call me back and we can cancel them'.

'OK, you can add them to my account', agreed the customer.

'And this is the new date for the installation of your new line. Can I help you with anything else?'

'No, thank you, you've been very helpful. You explained everything very well. Thank you again'.

'No problem sir. Thanks for calling Telemar'.

This was Themis' way of dealing with people. She usually managed to turn the conversation around, so a customer who started out being angry or rude would, by the end of the call, thank her for her help and even sign up for additional services. The great secret was patience. Obviously, there was an exception to every rule, and in this case, the exception had a name: Alegria Taiah – the terror of all customer service operators. In the late 1990s, it was such a complicated and expensive procedure to have a phone line installed at an address in Brazil that enterprising characters such as Mrs Taiah would invest vast sums of money in buying up phone lines and then rent them out – at great profit – to people living in homes without a pre-existing connection. Mrs Taiah had purchased hundreds of these lines and would call the customer helpline daily – usually to curse operators. This generally happened because she was extremely disorganised and sometimes did not know which line she had rented out to which address. As the operators were not able to make changes to customers' records without confirming their details first, they ended up having to listen to her foul-mouthed rants quite often. Themis herself had hung up on her several times after being the object of her outbursts.

Themis had always enjoyed working with the public. She liked talking to customers and finding a way to help them, even when the situation became complicated. She had received the 'Telemar Excellence' prize twice. The company had given out this prize over three consecutive months – October, November and December of 1999, and the only reason she didn't win in November was probably due to the fact that she'd been off work for two weeks after minor surgery that month. She remembered that time at Telemar, her work, colleagues, and the managers there, with great affection. She had been incredibly happy working there and even happier to receive the generous addition of luncheon vouchers at the end of the month. The company offered many such benefits until, sadly, it was privatised. It was not long after this happened that she left Telemar and moved to England.

Themis was close to home now, hoping that she might see a certain police car on her journey. *I wonder if I'll ever see Matt again?* She arrived at her door, but there was no little gift waiting for her today. It was the end of another working day, and although she had been surrounded by people all day, now that she was at home, lying on her bed, reality set in: she was alone.

CHAPTER 6

The American Backpacker

(The Best Croissant in the World)

Themis did not know if it was day or night outside the terminal. The English winter had arrived in all its splendour. Days had become shorter, and less than eight hours separated dawn from dusk. There were no windows in the immigration control area of Terminal D, which meant that officers working there would completely lose track of the time of day. She thought about how, if she were back in Brazil, she would be going to the beach at Leme at this time of year, celebrating her birthday and then, two weeks after that, Christmas. She was not feeling very Christmassy though; it did not have the same importance for her now that she was so far away from her family.

Themis had been sitting at her position in arrivals since 2:22 p.m. and, three hours later, was waiting for someone to come and take over. She was tired. She wanted to get out of there before the American flight arrived. She needed to go to the toilet and have something to eat!

'Hi boss, I've been sitting here for three hours. Can you send someone over to relieve me, please? I should have had my break an hour ago', said Themis, using the phone on the medical desk.

'Sorry, Themis. I've got a group of volunteers with me in the watch house. We're going to be training them here, in the terminal, over the next three weeks. Balder's just sorting out the officers who are going to be supervising them. I'll see if I can find someone to relieve you'.

'OK, thanks', said Themis, seeing the first of the American passengers start to filter through. *Why on earth are they sending in work experience people to train here? It's hectic enough as it is,* she thought.

'Hey lady, you OK?' asked a young man, walking towards Themis.

Oh no, here we go… another college boy, she sighed.

The refusal rate for young Americans was surprisingly high in the terminal. They finished their university studies and decided to travel the world, with no real direction and no money. They would get short-term, cash-in-hand jobs in British bars to cover their expenses when they ran out of money and their parents, who had already spent a fortune on their college education, stopped taking their calls asking for financial assistance. It most likely suited them to have their children out of reach of their wallets for a while. Themis already sensed that this traveller was going to end up among the terminal's statistics.

'Hi. Where have you travelled from today? Are you travelling alone?' she asked.

'I arrived in the UK from New York three months ago, but I went to visit my parents for Thanksgiving', he replied.

'I see... and what have you come back here for? I can see several entry stamps for the United Kingdom since August. What are you planning to do here?' asked Themis, who was getting more and more impatient with the young man. She did not know if she was thinking about her lunch break, which she had missed due to this passenger's arrival, or if she was worried she wouldn't be able to reach the bathroom in time.

'I'm taking time out from my studies for a year, and I thought I'd come and explore Europe', explained the young man.

Themis knew that these young people saw the United Kingdom, where they could earn higher wages due to the relative value of the currency, as a kind of 'base camp' for their travels. As soon as they had got enough money together, they would take off to other countries, to spend what they had earned working here illegally. When the money was spent, they would come back to London for another couple of weeks and repeat the cycle. This would go on for long periods, sometimes up to a year, between entries and departures. Under British immigration law, tourists were not permitted to stay in the United Kingdom for more than six months in any given twelve-month period, and working, whether paid or unpaid, was prohibited. One of the stamps in the young man's passport caught Themis' eye. A colleague had already told him that if he continued to come in and out of the country that way, he would eventually be refused entry.

'OK. Please go and sit in the waiting area. I need to make some checks', said Themis.

'Is there anything wrong?' asked the passenger.

'Yes. First, this stamp tells me you've been warned that you were spending a lot of time here. Is that correct?' asked Themis.

'Yes, but I've been out of the UK for two weeks…'.

'And second, if you don't mind, I need to do something that no one else can do for me. Please take a seat in the p… in the waiting area'.

Themis ran towards the nearest toilet, which was in the detention area. In order to reach it, she had to get through two doors that needed her to enter a whole lot of access codes to gain entry. They had just changed those codes and she still had not memorised them, so had to pull her diary from her bag.

Oh no, where did I write those codes down? Oh God, you have to push down two numbers at the same time on this one… What sort of a twisted mind dreamt this up? Whoever it was, they didn't think about people needing to get to the toilet in a hurry. Ahhh, finally! thought Themis, relieved to have made it into the cubicle in time.

With the most pressing of her problems resolved, Themis' thoughts turned to food. She often thought about the traditions of her European ancestors, particularly the culinary ones, and, more specifically, the meals her mother used to make: meatballs in tomato sauce, served with delicious, succulent pasta. There would be liberal amounts of sliced bread on the table, to soak up every last drop of sauce from the plate. The pasta was made at home from flour and eggs. Her mother did not need to worry about weights and measurements; she could create the most exquisite pasta just using her eye and experience. Themis could almost smell the tomato sauce, also home-made, bubbling away in the pan. Sundays back home were all about Mass in the morning, followed by some kind of pasta for lunch. The table would groan under the weight of various Italian and Portuguese dishes, drenched in delicious olive oil and washed down with wine. She remembered how Easter and Christmas were always marked with a fabulous *bacalhoada* – Portuguese dried cod with thinly sliced potato and onion, all in a delicious white sauce.

At the age of thirty-seven, her great-great-grandfather Giovanni had left the small town of Barco in northern Italy, together with his wife and their three children, all aged under ten. Just like Themis, they left behind everything they had ever known for an uncertain future in a foreign land, with their life packed into their suitcases.

They travelled through the mountainous terrain of northern Italy, crossed Switzerland and France, and finally arrived at the port of Le Havre. From there, it took them twenty to thirty days by a steam ship to cross the immense Atlantic and arrive in the New World: Brazil, the land of coffee. They were crammed into stinking cabins, and many fellow passengers perished – their bodies thrown into the sea – over the course of a long and painful journey. On 17th June, 1875, they saw land again for the first time, and after a stop-off in Rio de Janeiro, which was the capital of Brazil at that time, they disembarked in Piúma, in the state of Espírito Santo. Most of the passengers on the ship were land workers and had no idea about the path their lives were going to take until they arrived at their destination. From there, they were taken to immigrant hostels and then packed off to the farms where they would work from sunrise to sunset, until they had paid off their debt to the Brazilian government, who had very 'generously' covered the cost of their journey to Brazil.

Themis' father had also heard the call of the sea, leaving Portugal when he was still a young man, on the day before his seventeenth birthday. He made the same journey, also by ship, together with his older brother, who was twenty-two at the time. Their father, Themis' grandfather, had arrived in Brazil eight years earlier, leaving his wife and six children to fend for themselves in Portugal. He had promised that he would go back and get them one day, when he was earning enough money. Themis' father always told the story of the single roast sardine shared between six hungry children. Years passed by, and he never returned. The first thing the two brothers did upon their arrival in Brazil was to seek out their father's house and knock on his door. The reason why the patriarch had failed to return for them sooner became patently clear: he had a new family. Left to their fate on the streets of Rio de Janeiro, her father and uncle simply had to succeed; there was no other option.

Themis informed the chief immigration officer of her suspicions regarding the American backpacker, and he authorised her to carry out further enquiries. While Themis was going through the stages of her investigation, Balder, now standing near to the European control area, was instructing one of his new charges.

'Ok, this is the immigration control. On one side, we have the EU desks for passengers with European passports. On the other side, we deal with all the non-European passengers', explained Balder.

'How will I know the difference, though?' asked the trainee.

'Well, the ones with a red passport are usually from Europe. Look around you. What do you see?' asked Balder.

'Erm, loads of passengers?' the trainee replied to Balder's question with another of his own.

'All of these people are liars until they prove otherwise', said Balder, who offered these same words of wisdom to every new worker who passed through his hands. 'OK, let's go over to the European arrivals area. In this job, practice makes perfect'.

The pair remained there for almost two hours, which gave the volunteer an opportunity to see some of the different European passports in use.

'This passport is bright red. It's not a claret colour like the Italian passport', he noted at one point.

'That's right. Well spotted. This is a European passport as well – from Switzerland', explained Balder. 'So, what made you come and volunteer here anyway?' he asked the trainee. 'Not enough excitement in your life or what?'

'Sort of. Also, I think that some experience in immigration control will look good on my CV and create more opportunities for me in the future'.

The chief immigration officer came out of the

watch house to speak to Balder. 'Balder, Themis just stopped an American passenger – she's already prepared his file. Thing is, she's only got two hours before her shift ends, so that's not going to be enough time for her to get everything done. Do you mind taking over from her and letting her come and take your place here instead?' he asked.

'Yes, of course. Where is she?' asked Balder.

'She's on one of the computers, in the area near the changing rooms, at the back', replied the chief.

'On my way', Balder replied with a mock-salute to the chief immigration officer. He looked at the trainee and asked, 'Do you want to go and have a coffee while you wait for my colleague?'

'No, that's fine. I'll stay here. Don't worry. If I have any problems, I'll ask someone to rescue me', he joked.

Balder went to the back office and found Themis, who was getting ready to interview her passenger.

'So, Themis, what have you got for me?' he asked, smiling.

'Another one of those gap year students travelling around Europe and doing a bit of work in their spare time', she explained.

'The chief has asked me to take on the case, if that's OK with you, obviously', said Balder.

'Wonders will never cease! He must be feeling guilty for leaving me stuck at my desk for three hours without a break!' said Themis.

'Maybe, but, in return, you'll have to babysit the new boy for a couple of hours, until you finish your shift', laughed Balder.

'Yeah I can do that. Where is he?' she asked.

'Out there at the control. He said he didn't want to go for coffee'.

'But, Balder, didn't he only just start here this afternoon?'

'The other officers are helping him until you get there'.

'OK, no problem. I'm on my way. Oh, before I forget, I found what looks like a rota and salary payments scribbled on a piece of paper in the passenger's wallet. They look like hours worked. There's also a business card with the address of a pub on it', added Themis.

'Thanks, Themis. Have fun!' said Balder.

She quickly walked towards the control and noted that the flight from Moscow had just come in. As she approached the EU control, she saw a man with a Russian passport walk away from the desk of an officer.

'Excuse me, where have you just arrived from?' she asked the passenger.

'Moscow', he replied.

'Can I check your passport, please?' asked Themis.

She leafed through the document and saw that there were no stamps in it.

'Who let you in without checking your fingerprints and stamping your passport?' she thought out loud.

'It was me, but the passport is red! Balder told me that if they're red, they're European!' replied the trainee.

Themis thought she recognised the voice from somewhere. She turned and saw the police officer who had escorted her to the petrol station months ago, with the added bonus of blue lights included – the same man who had left a rose at her front door, which she had kept on her bedside table for days.

'Matt? What are you doing here?' asked Themis. She felt her face flush and did not know quite what to do with the passenger's passport.

The two looked at each other for a few seconds. It was a moment that seemed to last forever, and it filled Themis with a strange feeling of comfort and hope – as though the loose ends of her life were finally starting to come together.

She walked up to Matt's desk and explained to him that since Russia was not a member of the EU, all Russians needed a visa in order to enter the United Kingdom.

'You have to scan the passenger's passport and visa, take their fingerprints, and then, if they're good to enter, you need to stamp their travel document', explained Themis.

'OK, I get it now. There's only one problem. I haven't got a stamp. Can I borrow yours?' asked Matt.

'No way! You can't use somebody else's stamp!' she replied, still a little embarrassed by his presence.

Matt watched Themis as she questioned the passenger, took his fingerprints, stamped his passport, and then closed her desk.

'Themis, this is Matt. He's a police officer and has volunteered to help us out if we need extra bodies when things get busy', explained the chief immigration officer.

'Good to know, chief, but you told me they were on work experience. I didn't know they were police officers', said Themis.

'Yes, they're all police officers, Themis. You can go for lunch now if you like', he said.

'I think I might go for a coffee as well', said Matt, inviting himself along.

'OK, come with me. I'll introduce you to the best croissant in the world', said Themis. 'I'll just get my wallet from the locker, hang on a second'.

'No, this one's on me. Think of it as me trying to cancel out the terrible impression I just made with the Russian guy', said Matt, smiling.

In the café, they sat in awkward silence. Neither one seemed to know what to say to start the conversation.

'So, what made you decide to volunteer, Matt?'

'I needed to think of an excuse to meet up with you again', Matt confessed, not beating around the bush. 'I thought you didn't like my rose'.

'Matt, that's not what happened', she said, feeling herself tremble. 'I put your number in my pocket and then when I got home that night, I put everything in the washing machine without thinking. It was ruined, and I didn't have any way of getting in touch with you. Thank you for the lovely rose', she added, feeling a little flustered.

'No problem. The important thing is that we're here now, having a coffee and eating the best croissant in the world', he smiled. 'What are your days off this week?

'I took three days off – Friday, Saturday, and Sunday', she replied.

'Any particular reason?' he asked.

'It's my birthday on Saturday'.

'Great! Well, in that case, I'm going to take my days off at the same time', he said.

'That's great, but... what if the chief doesn't let you?'

'It's already done!'

'Oh... Anyway, we need to get back. The Air France flight is about to come in'.

'Come here. I'm not going to let you get away from me this time', said Matt, grabbing Themis' hand as she was getting up from her chair.

He fixed her with a penetrating and determined stare. She knew she could not escape from him now – not that she had the slightest intention of doing so. Just from the few moments she had spent in his company, she knew that they had a lot in common and felt a connection. They both chased their objectives single-mindedly and were rarely put off by obstacles appearing in their way.

'Have you got any plans for this evening?' he asked.

'Yes', she replied. 'I'm going to see "Rio" at the Bluewater shopping centre cinema. And before you invite yourself along, I should warn you that it's a kid's film'.

'Pick you up at half past nine?' he asked.

'OK', said Themis. 'But don't forget that it's a weeknight. We're back on duty at six tomorrow morning'.

'The night is young, Themis', he said.

The two of them walked back to the immigration control. Nothing else mattered to them in that moment – not even the queue of passengers that already extended to the international flight transfer desk.

Matt turned to her. 'Themis, have you seen that guy? He's been sitting next to the landing cards desk for some time now'.

'I hadn't noticed him. Why do you ask?' she replied.

'I first noticed him when Balder and I were sitting in the arrivals area. Then, we went for coffee and I saw him again, still sitting in the same place. He's still there now. I'm going to see what's going on. He's up to something', said Matt.

Themis followed Matt in the direction of the passenger. Matt suddenly lunged at the man, tearing from his hands the newspaper he was pretending to read. With the passenger's face now clearly visible, Themis could see that he had some wires attached to his body and electronic equipment in the pocket of his coat.

'What do you think you're doing?' asked Matt.

'Nothing. I'm not doing anything', replied the man.

Matt pulled on the wire to reveal a microphone and a camera hidden inside the man's coat.

'This is a restricted area. The use of electronic equipment is strictly prohibited here', he warned.

'I'm a reporter from Good Morning, *UK*. I'm working here', said the man.

Concerned that the situation could get out of control, Themis called the watch house on her mobile phone and asked for police enforcement.

'I don't care if you're a reporter. You're breaking airport security regulations. I'm confiscating your equipment, and it will be destroyed', said Matt.

Once the police enforcement arrived, Themis signalled to Matt that she was going back to her desk and then heading home after speaking to the chief. Matt waved back and called out for everyone to hear, 'See you later!'

Why does he keep embarrassing me like that? It's the second time he's done it! she thought, remembering the petrol station incident. She left the terminal and, after dropping off her security items in her locker, took the bus to the staff car park. It had started to snow, so she thought the cinema would probably have to wait for another day.

Back at home, Themis decided to get ready, just in case the crazy policeman did actually turn up. She put on jeans, a shirt, and a pair of leather boots. It was pretty cold outside. Then, she lay down on the sofa and started thinking about Matt and whether, one day, she would achieve the thing she wanted more than anything else in the world: to be a mother. Themis had always dreamed of having a big family seated around the Sunday dinner table, just like it had been back home in Brazil. Her parents' house was always full of people, bustling with energy. She had a brother and a sister, and there would invariably be a random selection of extended family members who turned up at the front door and ended up staying for months. Themis' father did not care; he loved having a full house. He owned a bar close to the beach at Leme and would bring home enough food to feed an army. Huge boxes of biscuits, whole legs of ham, big blocks of cheese – the fridge was always full, and no one ever went hungry. It was the same with all the Portuguese families she knew. They might not own the latest fashion in clothes and shoes, but they were never wanting for food. She missed being part of a family. Themis was just dozing off to sleep when the doorbell rang, and she jumped up from the sofa.

'You didn't think I'd turn up, did you? Ha! I never give up on a mission', said Matt. 'Are you ready?' he asked, coming into the house without waiting to be asked.

'I'll get my coat. Do you want a tea or coffee before we go?' asked Themis.

'No, but I'll take a kiss', said Matt, gently holding her face. 'May I?' he asked.

Themis gave him a kiss on the cheek and changed the subject, picking up her coat and house keys. They got into Matt's car and drove towards the shopping centre.

'I'm very pleased to see there are no blue lights on this car', she joked.

A smile played at Matt's lips. After he had pulled into a parking space at the shopping centre, he leaned into the back of the car and took a set of the very same blue lights from a compartment under the back seat. Themis realised that they were in an unmarked police car.

'Aren't you supposed to leave your car at the police station when you finish your shift?' she asked, surprised.

'I didn't have time. They only told me this morning that I was going to the airport. I'll take the car back tomorrow', he said, his eyes taking in every detail of Themis' face. 'I'm so happy I caught up with you again', he said after a long silence.

Matt embraced Themis and returned the kiss she had placed on his cheek earlier on that evening.

'The film's about to start', said Matt.

He held her hand throughout the film, while Themis explained to him the sights of her home city, Rio de Janeiro, which appeared in the film. He listened with interest. When the film had ended, they ate grilled chicken at Nando's – Themis' favourite restaurant. They even served the famous *pastel de nata,* a delicious Portuguese custard tart.

'So, what happened with the reporter?' asked Themis.

'He tried to attack me to get his equipment back. In the end, I had to arrest him, and we ended up at the airport police station', he told her.

'Wow! Good that you were there to stop him from filming us', said Themis.

They walked hand in hand back to the empty car park. Matt held the passenger door open for Themis to get in, and they drove back to her house.

'Themis, I'll come by and knock in a couple of hours, OK? There's no point taking two cars if we're both working the same shift', said Matt.

'OK. See you later then', she replied, getting out of the car.

She went into the house and had just enough time to have a shower, get a snack ready, and do her hair and make-up. She was glad she did not have to drive to the airport. She lay down on the sofa for a while, waking up only when she heard Matt's car pull up in front of the house. It was four in the morning.

'Morning Matt, are you OK? You're not too tired to drive, right?' asked Themis, concerned.

'No, I'm used to working long shifts. This is normal for me!' he laughed.

Themis fell asleep in the car and did not wake up again until they had arrived at the airport car park. When she opened her eyes, she realised that Matt had been watching her for some time.

'Sorry Matt, I was really tired', she apologised.

'I think you need another coffee!'

'You're not wrong!' said Themis.

They went into the Italian café and had breakfast together. It had been less than twenty-four hours since they had caught up with one another again, and yet it felt like they had been together their whole lives. Themis somehow felt remarkably close to him. She went to the locker room to leave her coat and pick up her stamp. She did not know if she would be at the desk or assigned to supervise Matt again. She went through the control on her way to the watch house and saw Matt and Balder talking. The impeccable supervisor had a smile on his face, which made Themis think that the two were up to something. She stamped the attendance book in the watch house and went back to the control.

'Morning, Themis', said Balder. 'Can you supervise our trainee after your break, from 10.30 to the end of your shift?' he asked.

'Yes, of course', she replied.

The trainees are doing a course on forged documents. It ends at ten', he explained.

Themis went back to her desk and saw that Matt was watching her from the other side of the control, as he walked to the training room with the other trainees. The airport was fairly busy. Themis took up her seat at the fast track fixed point, where she saw only those passengers who had flown first class.

'Passport, please'.

Themis knew she recognised the face of the man coming towards her, but she could not quite place him. He handed her his passport and she immediately understood why he had caught her attention. Inside the passport it read: *Surname: MANSELL / Name: Nigel Ernest James / Nationality:* GBR. She looked again at the famous passenger and realised that he no longer had his trademark moustache.

'Wow!', she involuntarily exclaimed.

He smiled but said nothing.

'Oh, if only you knew how much watching Formula 1 on Sundays meant to us Brazilians. You and Ayrton Senna. Obviously, we always supported Senna, but if his car broke down during a race, you always became our number one', said Themis, who still could not believe it was really him.

She would have really liked to have her photo taken with him but had to contain her excitement. He thanked her, took his passport back, and carried on through the gates.

The rest of the morning passed quickly. After her morning break, she met up with Matt and spent the rest of her shift with him, on the EU desk. Between passengers, they discussed Themis' unexpected encounter with the man who had been the second most successful British Formula 1 driver of all time, beaten to that honour only by his compatriot Lewis Hamilton. Matt told her about his training on forged passports and said that he had been quite taken aback by the degree of complexity involved in the work of immigration officers.

On their way home, Themis received a text message from Balder.

Hmph! What does he want now? I bet he wants to swap shifts for tomorrow... Themis thought.

The message read, 'Themis, I forgot to tell you before. Bring your passport tomorrow so we can register you on the new terminal security system. Don't forget!'

'Did they ask you to take your passport in tomorrow as well, Matt?' she asked.

'Yes', he replied.

'Themis, have you and Balder ever had a thing going on? He seems to really like you', Matt said.

'No, we're just good friends. I have a lot of respect for him. I nicknamed him the "Impeccable Supervisor", but he doesn't know that'.

The two laughed at Themis' confession. Matt dropped her off at her front door and set off to return the car to the police garage.

'I'll call you later, ok?' he asked.

'Great', she answered as she got out of the car.

Matt waited until Themis was safely inside the house before setting off towards the police station.

CHAPTER 7

The Meeting Place

*D*ear God! What day is it? What time is it?

Themis looked at the clock on the living room wall. It was 2:22 in the morning.

I must have lain down on the sofa and fallen asleep, she thought, feeling disorientated. She sat up, took her mobile phone out of her bag, and tapped in the security code. She noticed that the battery was practically empty.

Thursday, 9th December. Three missed calls from 'Matt the handsome policeman'. Themis laughed at the description she had saved his number under. She decided to change it to 'Matt the handsome boy-friend'. There were also two new text messages.

He must be worried about me, she thought. She decided she had better send him a message to let him know she was still alive. Seconds later, her phone rang.

'Hi, Matt. Sorry, I fell asleep and only woke up now. Are you OK? We're due in at eight today. Do you want me to pick you up from your place?'

'Morning, darling. I'm fine. I was just a bit worried about you, but I guessed you'd fallen asleep. I'll come around at six, is that OK?' he asked.

'Don't you ever sleep? I think it's better if we leave at five thirty. There can be a lot of traffic at this time of the day', said Themis, who was used to the ebb and flow of traffic on the M25.

'No problem. See you in a while. Don't forget your passport – and bring a change of clothes with you, so we can go for dinner when we finish work. What do you think? We can get the train into central London, maybe see the Christmas lights?'

'Ah, that's a lovely idea, Matt. OK, see you soon', said Themis. 'Now try and get some sleep!'

'Don't worry, I'm fine. Can't wait to see you'.

Themis was trying not to let herself get carried away by the possibility of this new relationship. She had been through some difficult experiences before and knew only too well that no one was perfect. She had been cheated on in the past by the person she loved the most in the world, and something like that left a mark that was not easy to erase. She had only just met Matt, and she reminded herself that she must not expect too much.

Themis put some warm clothes into a bag in preparation for the trip to London that evening. Make-up, deodorant, comb, scarf, gloves, and hat. Then she remembered she needed to take her passport. Once she had got everything ready, she decided that she might as well have a shower and get ready for work, as she knew she would not be able to get back to sleep.

Matt probably has the same problem as me. I think he has trouble sleeping, she thought. No matter how hard she tried, she could not stop hoping that things would work out for her this time, that it would be different.

How can I not fall for his personality, not to mention the fact that he looks gorgeous, she thought. Matt was very tall – easily over six feet – and was beautifully built. Themis had noticed this when he held her hand tightly as they were finishing their coffee on Tuesday, the first time they had met up again. He had green eyes, dark brown hair, and a three-day beard. At work at the airport, he had worn a suit and tie with formal shoes, although he took off the jacket during the day. He was not impeccable like Balder: his shoes were not always shiny, and he certainly did not bring in his suit on a hanger to stop it from getting creased. But there was definitely something very attractive about him. She had enjoyed seeing him in 'policeman' mode at the airport the previous day: tough and implacable, like Gene Hunt from 'Life on Mars'.

He will go all out to get the bad guys, thought Themis, *but he also has a caring side.*

The night before, at the shopping centre, he had caressed her hand all through the film, held it as they walked back to the car, and opened the car door for her. Deep down, Themis had really wanted him to kiss her when he left her at her door earlier that morning, but he had been a true gentleman. She chided herself for her thoughts.

Come on Themis, one day at a time! If it's meant to be, it will be! Yes, she was afraid, but she really hoped that this was the start of something wonderful. When he was around her, she felt as though all her defences had been stripped away – this was an unusual feeling for Themis who, helping control the country's borders at work, was more accustomed to showing off a tough, composed façade. But not when she was with him, not when she was with Matt. It was as though she could only be herself when she was by his side.

The doorbell rang earlier than she had expected it to. It was 5 a.m.

'Does that offer of coffee still stand?' asked Matt, presenting Themis with a flower. He kissed her on the forehead as he entered the house.

Themis was preparing coffee in an Italian coffee pot. She put some water in the bottom and some ground coffee in the filter.

'I've never seen a coffee maker like this one before', said Matt, looking at the pot on the stove.

'It's Italian', she explained. 'The water boils in the bottom part and then goes up through the filter. The coffee ends up in the top part'.

'Very odd', said Matt, not sounding convinced.

'Have you ever tried Brazilian coffee?' she asked.

'No, never, but it smells great', said Matt.

'Are you hungry?' asked Themis.

Matt responded with a smile.

She had some part-baked French sticks, bacon, sausage, tomatoes, and mushrooms in the fridge, and by a quarter past five, she had prepared Matt a full English breakfast.

'Erm, I don't want to be rude, but have you got any ketchup?' asked Matt, licking his fingers.

'Of course', said Themis, rather pleased that her breakfast had been met with his approval. *After all, she thought, if I'm going to seal the deal with him, I'll need to know how to make the basics of English cuisine.*

After eating, they left for the airport in a hurry. When they were on the motorway, Themis asked him, 'Are you going into London after work in your suit?'

Matt smiled and told her that he had a change of clothes in the boot of the car.

'Ah, OK', said Themis.

Matt held her hand for the entire journey. When he needed to change gear, he would take her hand and they would change the gear together. Every now and then, she noticed him taking his eyes off the road to look at her. There was hardly any traffic on the road that morning.

'Aren't you going to sleep a little?' he asked.

'I'm not tired, not after that coffee!' said Themis.

He parked the car. It was still only seven o'clock. They had an hour before their shift started. They watched the planes fly close over the airport employees' cars before coming to land a few metres ahead of them.

'Themis, when I saw you for the first time, sitting on that grass verge, next to your car, I felt something I'd never felt before. I can't explain what it was. It's still all very new to me. Please, the only thing I ask is that you open your heart and allow yourself to get to know someone new. I can tell you're afraid, and I don't know what happened to you in the past, but whatever it was, things are going to be different now', said Matt. His expression was serious, and he looked deep into her eyes. 'Themis, will you let me look after you?' he asked, as he stroked her face.

Themis did not say anything. They looked at each other without speaking.

They say that eyes are the windows to the soul, she thought. She felt the same way about him, and she could not hide it: her heart beat hard, and her mouth was dry. Matt held her face in his hands and gently kissed her on the mouth. They remained in an embrace for some time, each listening to the other's breathing. They both wanted this moment to last forever but knew that they had to get to work. Matt caressed her face once more and kissed her, followed by one last deep embrace.

As they got out of the car, the sun was coming up.

After the storm comes the calm, thought Themis. A new day was beginning – and, for her, a whole new phase in her life. They walked to the bus stop and made their way to the terminal. Matt held her hand all the way there.

'Passport, please. What is the purpose of your journey?' asked Themis, already counting the minutes until this shift ended and she had three full days ahead of her to spend with Matt.

'Tourism', replied the passenger.

Themis looked around the control and saw that Matt was dealing with the European travellers, under the supervision of Balder. They waved at her from across the hall, and she waved back, smiling.

She returned to her passenger. 'How long are you going to stay in the UK? Why are you travelling alone?'

'One week. My children couldn't come with me because they're still in school'.

'Who's looking after them?' asked Themis.

'My mum'.

Themis always tried to put herself in her passengers' shoes. So, here she had a woman in her thirties, who was travelling alone because her children were in school.

She left the children with her mother? Why not with their father?

She was not wearing a wedding ring. Her answers were vague, and she did not seem excited to be there on holiday.

If I were just arriving somewhere on holiday for the first time, I'd have maps, hotel reservations, information on all the sights that I was going to see... Themis thought

'What do you do in Brazil?' she asked.

'I work in an office', said the woman.

Themis noted down the woman's responses on the back of her landing card.

'What's your mother's name, please?'

'Dilma.'

'Can I have Dilma's phone number, please? And your work number? What's your boss's name?'

'I don't know my work number, but the company is called Administração Santini Ltda'.

After writing down all the details, Themis handed the passenger an IS81 form and walked over to Balder and Matt.

'It looks like I'm going to have to do a refusal, so I won't be able to stay and help out here', she said, looking at Matt. 'Oh, Balder, before I forget, here's my passport. I'll see you both later. Look after the new boy and make sure he doesn't get his red passports mixed up again!' she laughed.

The men laughed, and Matt winked at Themis. She smiled; she knew she was unlikely to see him again until the shift ended, because she would be spending the rest of the day working on this case. She went to the watch house and then the back office to use the phone.

'Could I speak to Dilma, please?'

'Who is this?' asked the woman, sounding slightly worried.

'Hi Dilma, my name is Themis. I'm an immigration officer at an airport in London. Don't worry, your daughter has arrived safely, but I need to ask you a few questions. Is that OK?'

'Yes, of course, dear', said the woman, still half asleep.

'How long is Denise planning to stay in London?'

'I don't know for sure'.

'Does she have any children?'

'She does, yes'.

'How old are they?'

'One's eight, and the other is ten'.

'Where is their father? Why didn't they come to London with their mum?'

'They're separated. The kids' father has never really been that involved with them. Denise lost her job last week, so she decided to try her luck over there'.

'I understand. So, your daughter didn't come here for a holiday?'

'No dear, she's going to try and get some cleaning work. She's got a friend who lives in London, and she said she'll help her find some work cleaning people's houses'.

'That's great, Dilma. Thanks very much. And my apologies for calling so early in the morning'.

Themis hung up and realised that she would not be able to call the woman's employer yet, as it was only six o'clock in the morning in Brazil. She did, however, have enough information to justify checking her bags. She went to the watch house to inform the chief immigration officer of the details of the case and then went back to collect Denise and take her to the baggage claim area, passing Matt's desk on her way to the first floor.

'Very good work, Themis', said Balder, his voice laced with irony.

'Shut up, Balder!' she shot back, laughing.

Blowing her a kiss from behind Balder's back, Matt called out to her, 'Good luck, Themis'.

On the first floor, Themis helped Denise take her case from the baggage carousel and walked to the customs inspection area, where all the bags were checked.

'You only brought one case?'

'Yes', replied Denise.

Themis noted that the woman had only brought a few clothes with her, but among her belongings was a diary. Themis immediately confiscated this and placed it in a folder for a more detailed analysis later.

'Which part of Brazil are you from?' she asked.

'Londrina, in Paraná'.

Londrina, or 'little London', was named after the English capital. The city originally came about as a result of the colonisation of the northern region of the state of Paraná, in the deep south of Brazil, by an English company, which came to be the biggest producer of coffee in the world in the 1960s. The British introduced railways to Brazil, initially to make the transportation of coffee easier. Other cities sprang up along the railway line, leading to the development of the entire northern part of the state, and the rail network itself created an important connection between the southern and the south-eastern areas of Brazil. The red phone boxes more commonly associated with Londrina's English namesake can still be found throughout the city, and the main shopping centre is decorated with a London theme, depicting iconic figures such as the Queen's guards and Big Ben. Another interesting fact is that the national dialling code for some towns around Londrina is 44 – the same as the international dialling code for the United Kingdom.

Leaving Denise in the holding room, Themis went to prepare her file. By now, it was almost eight o'clock in Brazil, and, having already found the phone number of Denise's workplace through an online search, she made the call.

'Administração Santini Ltda., how may I help you?'

'Good morning, could I speak to someone in Human Resources, please?'

'Of course. Please hold while I transfer your call'.

'Human Resources, how can I help?'

'Hello, my name is Themis, and I work for the British immigration service. I have a passenger here who is requesting entry into the United Kingdom as a tourist and she told us she works for your company. Would you be able to confirm this?'

'Of course. Can you please give me her full name and date of birth?'

Themis had taken Denise's documents from her wallet but left all the money in there. She had written on the form that the woman had fifty pounds in sterling, along with two hundred Brazilian *reais* – just under thirty pounds – and some loose change.

Themis read out the passenger's details to the woman on the other end of the phone, who confirmed what Dilma had already told her: Denise had been working for the company until the previous week, but only on a temporary contract. The woman confirmed that she was no longer a part of their team.

'Thank you very much for your help. Have a good day', said Themis, as she ended the call.

So, besides not having a job, she's got no money and no real reason to return to Brazil after her visit, Themis concluded. She leafed through the diary that she had found in the passenger's case. The last entry was from 8th December. Denise had written, 'A new life starts for me today. I'm moving to London'.

Back in the interview room, Themis went through the initial security questions and then started interviewing the passenger.

'What is the purpose of your journey?'

'As I said before, tourism', she replied.

'What are you planning to see in England?' asked Themis.

'As much as I can fit into seven days'.

'Do you have a job in Brazil?'

'Yes'.

'What is your monthly salary?'

'About a thousand *reais*'. Themis did a quick mental calculation – it was less than a hundred and forty pounds.

How much did you pay for the flight?'

'Three and a half thousand *reais*'.

'So, let me get my head round this', said Themis. 'You have spent more than three times your monthly salary to fly to London – a place you know nothing about – for just one week?'

'Yes'.

'I spoke to your mum, Dilma, earlier. She told me that you no longer had a job there, as you have been laid off. She also told me that the father of your children did not provide any financial assistance for them. Then, she told me that you had come to London to work as a cleaner, that you had a friend who lived here and that she was going to help you find some clients. What can you tell me about that?'

'My mother's crazy. She doesn't know what she's talking about', said the woman, starting to get angry.

'And the people at your workplace are crazy as well? I called the company you said you worked for. I spoke to the personnel department, and they confirmed that your employment had been temporary and that it came to an end last week. Oh, and on top of all this, you wrote in your diary that you were going to start a new life in London'.

'I'm not going to answer any more questions. You can send me back if you want', Denise aggressively said.

'That's exactly what I'm going to do', Themis bluntly stated. 'You've lied to the British immigration service, and you had every intention of working here illegally. I am afraid you are being refused entry on this occasion. You will not be able to return to the United Kingdom for the next ten years. Do you understand everything I have told you?'

'Yes!' Denise shouted.

'Please sign here', Themis patiently asked. 'Thank you. If you want anything to eat, just ask the security guards. Have a nice day', she said, relieved that the interview was over.

She gave a summary of the interview to the chief immigration officer, who, in turn, agreed with Themis that Denise should be refused entry. Her phone beeped: it was a message from Matt, saying that he was waiting for her outside the terminal, in the Italian café. Themis did not know where the time had gone. It was already half past three, and she should have finished her shift by now. She completed Denise's file and handed it to the Duty Office, so they could sort out her return flight. She sent Matt a message, telling him she was on her way, placed her security items in her locker, next to her personal stamp, and quickly retouched her make-up and changed out of her uniform. Twenty minutes later, she walked towards the arrivals area, where Matt was anxiously waiting for her.

'Hi, everything OK?' asked Matt, happy to see her again.

'Yes. You?' asked Themis, tired but also happy.

'How was your shift? Did you refuse that passenger in the end?'

'It was a bit stressful. She was refused, yes. She came here to work, but she didn't have a work visa', replied Themis.

Matt put his arm round Themis, and the couple walked towards the ticket office of the airport's train station. They took the express train to Paddington, and in fifteen minutes, they were in the heart of London. From there, they took the tube to King's Cross/ St. Pancras station. This is famous for 'Platform 9¾' from the Harry Potter films and the international St. Pancras platform from which the Eurostar trains leave to travel to cities in Holland, France, and Belgium. There are many restaurants and a shopping centre at the station, which is at walking distance from the British Library.

They entered the huge station concourse, and Matt led Themis to look at a beautiful bronze sculpture called 'The Meeting Place', next to the international departure platforms. This statue, nine metres high, was designed by the British artist Paul Day and alludes to the romance of travel, with its representation of a couple in a loving embrace.

'Themis, I have a surprise for you. I know I said I was going to take you for a meal in London, but that is not actually true... We're going to eat on board the Eurostar to Paris. Our train leaves in an hour. We're coming back on Sunday. Is that OK?' smiled Matt.

'But... Matt, I didn't bring enough clothes for three days! I haven't even got my passport with me!'

Matt took two passports from his coat pocket. Themis did not know what to say, and they embraced under the bronze statue.

'I can't believe you managed to trick me like that!'

'I couldn't have done it without Balder's help!' laughed Matt.

'Ah Matt, you've brought a little bit of sunshine into my life. Thank you', said Themis.

'Themis, we're going to have an amazing weekend. This is going to be one birthday you'll never forget – I promise you. Don't worry about clothes. We can do some shopping tomorrow in Paris'.

Themis embraced Matt and, holding his face in her hands, kissed him. 'I love my surprise', she murmured in his ear.

They walked to the boarding queue and then waited in the cocktail bar for their platform to be announced. Themis had never travelled in business class on the Eurostar before. Once on the train, they settled into their spacious seats, with a table to themselves, and were welcomed on board with a bottle of Duval Leroy champagne. Thirty minutes into the journey, dinner was served. The first course consisted of a selection of French cheeses, accompanied by bread rolls, a biscuit selection and apricot chutney.

'We'll be passing by our houses soon', said Matt.

'Yes. You know, Matt, I really like where we live, in the countryside. Life isn't as hectic there as it is in the city. After dealing with so many passengers every day, it's nice to go back home to somewhere peaceful'. said Themis.

'My love, if you like living in Kent, then we'll stay there'.

Themis did not know how to reply to this. Nevertheless, she was glad to hear that Matt had plans for their relationship beyond the weekend together in Paris.

'Do you like your job, Themis?' he asked.

'Hmm... I think it's a very important job, but it's the type of thing that can leave you with, I don't know, bad energy. If you think about it, we're changing people's lives with every decision we make. I know that it's an essential job, but I don't think it's something I want to do forever. Sometimes, I think I'd be happier helping people', said Themis.

'Yeah, I get that. I think it's important to do something you enjoy. And anyway, who's going to look after the children while I'm out chasing baddies?'

'Ah, you've got a point there!' agreed Themis, snuggling closer to Matt, who had taken off his thick winter coat.

After the starter, they were served the main meal: duck à l'orange, followed by a delicious chocolate mousse, and an espresso to finish.

'I prefer the coffee you make for me', said Matt.

'I'll make you another when we get back on Sunday', she promised.

A taxi was waiting for them when they arrived at the Gare du Nord. After checking into the hotel where they were going to spend the next three nights, they went straight up to their room. Themis could hardly contain her excitement; she could not wait to go out and see the sights, in particular the Eiffel Tower. When they entered the room, she went to the balcony and gasped at the sight of the golden lights of the tower winking back at her. Matt came up and embraced her from behind, and the pair stood and admired the beauty of Paris in the night-time.

'Matt, can I say something?' asked Themis in a low voice, almost a murmur.

'Themis, I love you too', he whispered in her ear. 'Now, it's my turn. Can I ask you something?'

'Of course you can ask me something, Matt, and the answer is yes! – to both your questions', she said, looking deep into his eyes.

They kissed for a long time. At last, Themis felt safe. They spent Friday and Saturday looking at the sights of Paris. Matt asked the head chef at the hotel to prepare a cake especially for Themis on her birthday. When they got back to their room on Saturday night, it was full of red roses and there was a cake with strawberries and a bottle of champagne on the table. Themis made a wish as she blew out the candles: she wanted to be by Matt's side forever. On Sunday, they had breakfast in their room, looking out over the icy streets below them, before packing their bags and saying goodbye to Paris. A taxi was waiting for them at the entrance to the hotel.

'Charles de Gaulle airport, please', Matt told the driver.

'What? Are we going back by plane?' asked Themis.

'Yes, I thought it was more practical given that my car is at the airport carpark already', explained Matt.

'You really think of everything, don't you?' she said, smiling. 'This weekend has been unforgettable.

Everything was perfect. I think it's been my best birthday ever. Thank you, Matt'.

'I've loved spending time with you as well. It's going to be so difficult not seeing you tomorrow. I'm on a police training course all day, but I guess we can see each other in the evening'.

'I'll miss you too', replied Themis.

The flight from Paris to London only took around forty minutes. From the air, Themis and Matt could see the Medway River – which ran close to their homes – making its way to meet the Thames. They got off the plane at Terminal D and prepared their passports for immigration control.

'Matt, do you know what immigration officers hate most of all? Even more than the Italian paper ID documents?'

'What's that, Themis?'

'Passport covers! Take that cover off! Didn't you learn that on the document forgery course? It's especially important that we examine the cover of the passport!' laughed Themis.

'Oh God, you're absolutely right!' said Matt, quickly removing the leather cover from his passport.

As they approached the desk, Matt said, 'Look, Themis, it's Balder! Let's go through his lane!'

'Passport, please. Where are you travelling from? How do you know each other?'

Matt handed the two passports to Balder. 'We're arriving from Paris. And this is my future wife', he replied with conviction.

'Matt! Stop it!' said Themis, squeezing his hand.

'But you said yes to both questions!' he reminded her with a smile.

'Honestly, you two are a right pair. Themis, don't try to hide it; the whole airport knows that you're to-gether!' laughed Balder, adding fuel to the flames.

Themis went bright red as the two walked on, hand in hand. This was the third time that Matt had embarrassed her in front of everyone. She guessed she was going to have to get used to it. They went through the baggage hall, but as they had not checked in any bags, they walked straight through, towards the exit. Matt drove Themis home, and parking outside her house, he said, 'How about a coffee from that funny little Italian coffeemaker?'

'No problem', she said, hugging him tightly.

They talked for hours, and Matt ended up spending the night at Themis' house. He jumped out of bed at five the next morning. Themis was working on the quarter-to-two shift and would be dealing with the direct flight from Brazil. She knew that she had an exceptionally long day ahead of her. Matt kissed her and left her in bed to sleep a little longer.

'I finish at nine tonight, but it might be a bit later if I have to deal with any refusals. Is that OK?' asked Themis.

'No problem. I'll come over as soon as you get here', said Matt.

'Here, take the spare key and let yourself in. You can wait for me'.

'OK, great. Sleep a bit more, Themis. I love you', he said softly.

'I love you too', she said sleepily, wrapping the covers around herself.

CHAPTER 8

The Indian from Rio Negro

It felt strange for Themis to be leaving the house on her own that Monday morning. She and Matt had been together for less than a week, but she had never felt so sure about anything. It just felt right. A new week at work was beginning, and she felt as though her batteries had been recharged. She took her stamp from her locker and, as soon as she walked into the control, was intercepted by the chief immigration officer on duty that day.

'Afternoon, Themis. How are you? Listen, the Brazilian flight arrived early today, and we have got a passenger waiting for you in the pan. From what I understood from the interpreter, she came to the United Kingdom to have some sort of a medical procedure that is illegal in Brazil'.

'An abortion?' asked Themis, horrified at the idea.

'Yes', replied the boss.

'Why is it always me who has to deal with these cases? I'm sure one of the other officers could do it instead!' she protested.

'Because I decided that you're the best person to deal with her. She's pregnant, and she doesn't speak English. It's as simple as that', replied her boss.

'OK, but I'm telling you now that I'm going to refuse her entry', said Themis, not at all happy with the situation.

'You'll follow the standard procedure, Themis. She's in the pan, waiting for you', said the chief as he turned and walked away towards the watch house.

Themis watched the passenger from a distance. She remembered the agony she had been through in her attempts to get pregnant. She had been newly married and was still living in Brazil when she received the diagnosis of endometriosis and polycystic ovary syndrome. Every month, she had to cope with the painful reminder that she was unable to get pregnant and that she would never be a mother, and this made her feel that she was not 'complete' as a woman. It was literally painful too: excruciating cramps that nothing seemed able to relieve, until a friend put her in touch with a gynaecologist she trusted. At her first appointment, driven to desperation by the pain, she arrived at the clinic with one thing on her mind: she just wanted to get rid of everything that was causing her that suffering.

'So, doctor, do you know what it is?' she asked him.

'Yes, I think so. From the symptoms you describe, I am almost certain that you have endometriosis, but we're going to have to do a video laparoscopy to confirm it'.

'What's endometriosis? What's a video laparoscopy? Is it some sort of examination?'

'Endometriosis is a disease in which cells migrate from the endometrium – that's basically the lining of the womb – to other parts of the body, outside of the womb, and this then causes inflammation, pain, and, very often, infertility. To find out if this is the case with you, we need to examine your pelvic area by video laparoscopy. It's a surgical procedure'.

'All that just for a diagnosis, doctor? I need to get this sorted once and for all. Can you not just take out my womb and get it over with? Please, I can't cope with any more of this', begged Themis. She was only twenty-three at the time.

'Themis, I can't do that. You just got married and you told me that you wanted to have children. Stay calm. Trust me, you are in good hands', said the doctor.

She had all the pre-operative tests and, many times, thought about giving up. Two months later, she underwent surgery, remaining in hospital for just one night. Within two weeks, she was back at work. As part of the treatment, when the diagnosis had been confirmed, the doctor prescribed an injection called Zoladex. The needle was the size of a Bic ballpoint pen refill and each injection cost the equivalent of a month's salary for Themis. She needed to have one injection a month for six months and did not have the money to pay for the treatment. A good friend paid for three injections with her credit card, and Themis eventually managed to get the remaining three from the Brazilian equivalent of the NHS. She would administer these horrible injections herself, in her abdomen. She had no periods for six months, but the side effects of the drug were unpleasant: difficulty sleeping, hair loss, night sweats, and extreme irritability. It was like having PMT constantly for six months. The final straw was when, in the middle of all this, she found out that her husband was having an affair and that the other woman was pregnant. Themis had blamed herself for her misfortune; she managed to convince herself that she had failed as a woman and as a wife. It was at this point that she decided to leave it all behind and start afresh in another country – a new life with everything she had ever desired: a home, a husband, and a baby.

Now, she found herself looking across a room at this young girl who wanted to get rid of the thing Themis desired most in the world: the opportunity to create a new life and watch over it until the end of her days. From behind, the passenger appeared to be a young Brazilian–Indian woman. She had long, beautiful black hair and dark skin. She was short and slim, and it was not until she stood up and approached Themis' desk that her bump was visible.

This threw Themis off guard for a few seconds, but she composed herself and started the initial interview. 'What is the purpose of your journey?'

'To have an abortion', replied the young girl almost automatically, showing no emotion at all. It was as if she had learnt a script and was just reciting the words. Her face was pale, and she had a faraway look in her eyes.

'How many weeks along are you?' asked Themis.

'Twenty-three to twenty-four weeks', replied the girl.

Themis felt sick. She did not want to be there. She thought about asking permission to leave, but she knew she had to stay. She had to stop this from happening.

'We're going to need to check your case. Please come with me'.

On the short journey to the baggage hall, she prayed for divine intervention in this case. She knew that, legally, she needed some kind of proof to deny the woman entry. She prayed that she found something in her case that would justify refusing her. The woman had brought just one large travel bag with her, and inside it, there were some clothes, various documents relating to her pre-natal care, and some letters from her doctor. Themis took all the documents and put them in the passenger's folder. They went back to the immigration control and then to the holding room. She left the woman with the immigration assistants, who would take her fingerprints and a photo. While this was being done, Themis went to the office to examine the documents she had found in the young woman's bag.

There were some ultrasound scans and results of blood tests, but it was a letter that really caught Themis' attention. It was a recent document, prepared just three days earlier. In it, the doctor had listed the patient's medical condition and certified the gestational age of the baby: The young girl was twenty-four to twenty-six weeks pregnant.

That's it! In the United Kingdom, terminations can only be carried out up to a maximum of twenty-four weeks' pregnancy!

The young woman would not be able to have the procedure here, or anywhere else for that matter. This information took a huge weight off Themis' shoulders. Now, she felt confident that there would be a favourable outcome to this case – not so much for the passenger, but for the baby she was carrying. She called the watch house to update the chief on the case so far, then went to the holding room to carry out the full interview.

'Good afternoon, Isis. Are you OK? Please come with me to the interview room', she said. 'Have you had anything to eat? Do you feel well enough to answer some questions?'

'Yes, I'm fine', replied the pregnant woman. 'How long am I going to have to stay here?'

'Well, at least until after we've finished the interview. Then, I'll give a summary of your answers to my manager, and we'll decide whether to give you permission to come into the country or if you'll have to go back to Brazil', explained Themis.

'I understand, but have you spoken to my fiancé? He's outside, waiting for me', said the girl.

'If we need to talk to him as part of the procedure, then, yes, we'll interview him as well', said Themis, before moving on to start her questions.

'Please tell me why you decided to travel to the United Kingdom?'

'I'm pregnant, and we want to have an abortion', she replied.

'When you say "we", who do you mean?' Themis asked.

'My fiancé and I'.

'Is it a boy or a girl?' asked Themis.

After the briefest of pauses, the young woman placed her hands on her belly and answered, 'It's a girl', caressing her bump unconsciously.

Themis immediately realised that the young woman had an emotional link with her baby. *Something here isn't making sense,* she thought. She was certain of one thing, though: Isis did not want to get rid of her baby.

'Why did you wait six months before coming here? Is someone forcing you to do this?' she asked.

'My fiancé bought a ticket almost every month so that I could come here, but every time, at the last minute, I decided not to come. He finally said that he'd leave me if I didn't go through with the abortion'.

'But you're only eighteen… What do your parents think of all this?' asked Themis.

'They don't approve. My mum isn't talking to me; she didn't even come with me to the airport', replied Isis.

'Isis, here, in the United Kingdom, you can only have a termination up to the twenty-fourth week of pregnancy; that's the limit. I found a letter from your doctor, written last Friday, and it indicates that your pregnancy has already gone beyond that period. Unfortunately, I'm going to have to refuse you entry on this occasion'.

'But my fiancé will end things with me. You can't do this. Please, let me come in', pleaded the young woman, crying now.

'Isis, I'm the one that's not letting you in. You did what you could by travelling here. It's not your fault. And to be honest, if your fiancé ends the relationship now, then he would probably have done it anyway at some point. I'm going to talk to my manager. The final decision is for him to make but I should tell you that I'll be recommending a refusal. I'll be back to talk to you in a while'.

Themis went to the watch house and explained the young woman's situation to her chief. He agreed with Themis – that she did not fulfil the pre-requisites for entry into the United Kingdom as a visitor, and they decided to issue her a refusal. Themis went to the back office to type her interview notes into the system, and when she was almost done, she heard her name being called over the loudspeakers, asking her to contact the watch house. She called her boss, who informed her that the passenger's sponsor wanted to talk to her in the external interview room.

In Terminal D, there was a room that had a glass partition dividing it – one side of this partition was considered as being 'airside', and this was where the immigration officer would sit. The other section was 'landside', and the family member or sponsor would remain there. There was no access door enabling physical contact between the parties on the two sides.

'How can I help you?' asked Themis as she sat down, holding a pen with no lid and a piece of paper to take down the details of the interview. Everything that was said between the parties, whether face to face or over the phone, was written down in the passenger's file.

'I want to know why you're not letting my fiancée in', asked the man brusquely.

'We're refusing your fiancée entry because she doesn't fulfil the pre-requisites to enter the United Kingdom as a visitor for medical treatment. She told us that she was coming here to have an abortion. The thing is, it isn't possible for this procedure to be carried out when the pregnancy is over the twenty-four-week stage'.

'But I don't want *that thing!*' the man shouted, punching the thick protective glass.

'Sir, please calm down, or I'll have to call the police to remove you from the airport'.

'You can't do this! You can't!' shouted the passenger's fiancé.

'Sir, not only can I do it, but I am doing it. And, for your information, my manager has already signed your fiancée's refusal documentation. There's nothing I can do to change the outcome of this case. Thank you.', said Themis, getting up from her chair.

'You're going to regret this!' the man threatened Themis.

'This interview is over. Good evening', she said, leaving the room.

Themis felt a little intimidated, but she knew she was doing the right thing. She had been through a similar situation before, in the very same room, when a man had threatened to kill himself after she had refused his girlfriend entry. The sponsor had stood up and very determinedly told her that he was going to throw himself under the next express train. After she had reported the incident to the chief immigration officer, the airport police were contacted. Themis and the police officers conducted a search of Terminal D and found the sponsor hiding in one of the toilets. The chief immigration officer, as a precaution, ended up allowing the woman temporary entry. She was supposed to return to the airport a few days later, but just absconded.

The encounter with the young woman's sponsor had left Themis shaken. She would need an escort to the car park that night when she finished work. She wished Matt were there.

Themis went back to the office to finish her notes and soon heard another message for her over the loudspeaker:

'Themis, please contact the watch house immediately. Officer Themis, please contact the watch house.'

Oh no, she thought, what now? I'm never going to get this case finished with all these interruptions...

'Hi, Themis here. You asked me to get in touch?' she asked.

'Themis, I just had a call from the security staff in the holding room, saying that your passenger isn't well. Can you go there straight away, please?'

'Chief, this is going to be about her fiancé. He went ballistic when I told him she'd been refused', explained Themis.

'Even so, please go and check on how she is', asked the chief.

'OK. On my way'.

When Themis arrived in the holding room, she could see that the young woman was talking to someone on the public payphone. As soon as she noticed Themis, she hung up.

'How can I help you, Isis?'

'I'm not feeling well', the young woman replied.

'Have you spoken to your fiancé?' asked Themis.

'Yes, he's furious', she replied.

'If you're not feeling well, we can get you escorted to the local hospital. But you'll be brought back to the airport after the doctor is done with you. In any case, there's no changing the decision now. What do you want to do?'

'If it really can't be changed, then I'd rather go back to Brazil today', said Isis.

'Did he threaten you?' asked Themis.

'He told me to tell you I wasn't feeling well, to see if you'd let me come in'.

'So, are you OK?' repeated Themis.

'Yes, I feel fine, but I'm very tired'.

'Good. Please sign here to confirm what you've just told me. You're absolutely sure that you're feeling alright?' Themis asked her again.

'Yes, I'm fine', said Isis, signing the declaration.

'OK. Get some rest. Don't speak to him again until you are back in Brazil. It'll be better for you. I'll do everything I can to get you on the next flight'.

She went back to the office to complete the outstanding paperwork and remembered that she still needed to contact the airline company, so that they could reserve the young woman's return seat. She decided to do this in person and walked over to the airline's reservation desk. Themis knew most of the staff by their first names, as she refused a lot of passengers at the terminal.

'Hi, Gabriel, I'm happy it's you on duty today!' she said as she approached the desk.

'How can I help you, Themis?' he asked.

'Gabriel, I'm dealing with a very vulnerable passenger at the moment, and I was wondering if you could help me. She's been travelling since yesterday. She left Manaus with a stopover in São Paulo and then on to London. She's twenty-four weeks pregnant but is feeling OK. We've refused her entry, and that's why I'm here really – first, to reserve the return flight and second, to find out if... well, to ask if you could put her in executive class? Please?' asked Themis.

'Ha! I think you might be pushing your luck a bit there, Officer Themis! Give me a minute. Let me see what I can do for you', he said.

As she waited for Gabriel to check the available flights, Themis sent Matt a message. It was already almost nine, and her shift was supposed to be ending soon. She knew, however, that she was not getting out of there anytime soon. The return flight to Brazil was scheduled for ten, but it was already showing on the screens as being delayed until at least eleven o'clock. Her phone rang: It was Matt.

'Hey darling, how are you? I miss you', he said.

'I'm OK, but it's been a tough shift. I was threatened by some guy during an interview in the external interview room', she told him.

'I'm on my way'.

'Thanks, but there's no need. By the time I finish, it's pretty unlikely that he'll still be around. Anyway, I've already told the chief'.

'Themis, I said I'd come and pick you up. Don't leave the terminal until I get there'.

'OK, but drive carefully. I won't be done for another two hours', said Themis, feeling concerned.

'I'm leaving now. See you in a while. Love you'. Matt hung up immediately.

'Themis, I managed to reserve a seat for your passenger. In executive class, just like you asked!' said Gabriel.

'Ah, that's fantastic! Gabriel, you're a real angel. You don't know how much you've helped me! Thank you!' said Themis.

She went back to the holding room and told Isis that everything was sorted out for her flight back home and that it was scheduled to leave in two hours' time.

'Isis, my shift has ended now, but I'm going to stay here until your flight departs, OK? Try and rest a little. I'll be back in an hour. Do you want anything to eat?' she asked.

'Thanks, I'm not hungry. I just can't wait for this nightmare to be over', said the girl, evidently relieved.

'It's all going to be OK, don't you worry', Themis reassured her.

Themis went to the watch house to update the night shift chief immigration officer, who had just taken over the duties, of the details of the case and the steps she had taken to ensure the passenger's wellbeing. She also informed him of the threat that the passenger's sponsor had made during the interview. She went to the back office to finish off the case file and prepared to escort Isis to her flight. Themis stamped her passport and then drew a cross over the stamp, to show that she had been refused entry.

'Are you ready, Isis?' asked Themis, entering the waiting room.

'Yes', replied the young woman.

'OK. These two gentlemen in fluorescent jackets are your escorts. I'm coming with you as well. I don't usually do this, but I wanted to make sure you got on the plane'.

The four of them walked to the departure lounge, where the other passengers were already waiting. Once they had all boarded the plane, it was Isis' turn. The escorts had already checked her in and received her boarding pass. Her passport was handed to the captain, and there was nothing more to do now but take the young Indian girl back to the place where her journey had begun.

'Isis, when all of this is behind you and you look back at what happened today, I hope you don't see it as a door closing, but as a new window opening in your life. Remember, we refused you entry today partly because you didn't meet the legal requirements for entry, but, more than anything, because we're obliged to make sure that visitors to our country are safe', explained Themis.

'I understand. And thank you for saving my little Irene's life. That's going to be her name', said the girl, her eyes filling with tears as she hugged Themis. Isis turned towards the door of the plane, but before she entered, she looked at Themis and, caressing her belly, said to her, 'She'll be your daughter too!' She waved goodbye to Themis, and then she was gone.

Themis felt proud of her work that day, and proud that she was able to save a life. She really did feel like she would be a second mother to the little miracle, Irene, who would be born by Rio Negro – the largest blackwater river in the world, in the Amazon region; and although the baby would not come from her own womb, she felt that, in some way, they would have a connection for the rest of their lives. For the first time, Themis forgave herself for her personal failure, as she saw it, for being incomplete as a woman.

Themis suddenly understood what her purpose in life was. The paths she had travelled to get to this point – the doubts she had, the knowledge acquired along her journey, the daily struggle to achieve the freedom she had sought since leaving her beloved Brazil, her dreams of working in this job since that moment of arrival in the United Kingdom, seeing her

most intimate possessions strewn over a customs inspection desk! All this had led to where she was now. None of her efforts had been in vain. All the past experiences – good and bad – had created the Themis who stood there now, in the doorway of that plane. Tears flowed down her face, but they were happy tears, born of relief and a sense of accomplishment. When the plane door closed, she turned and saw Matt standing behind her. He put his arms around her and wrapped her in a tender embrace.

'Are you ready now, Themis?' he asked.

'Yes', she said with a smile.

'Let's go home', he said, taking her by the hand.

SAO PAULO
AIRPORT
THE END
ARRIVED

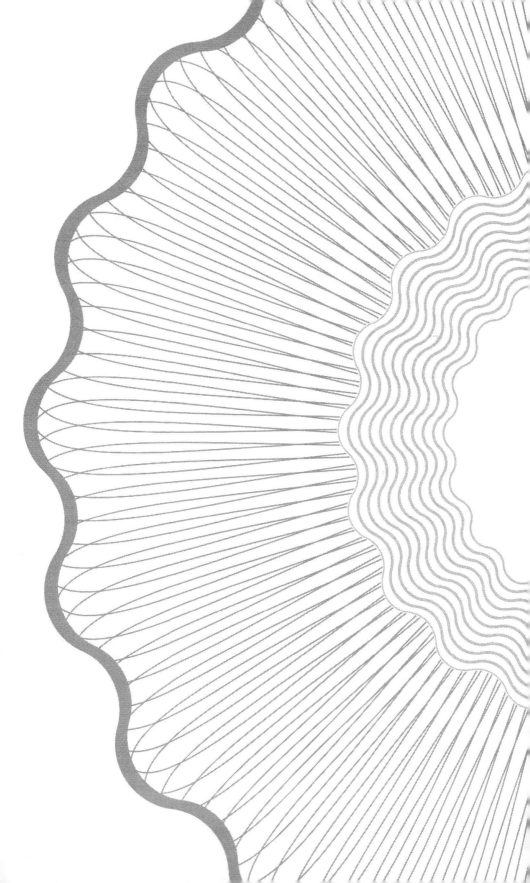

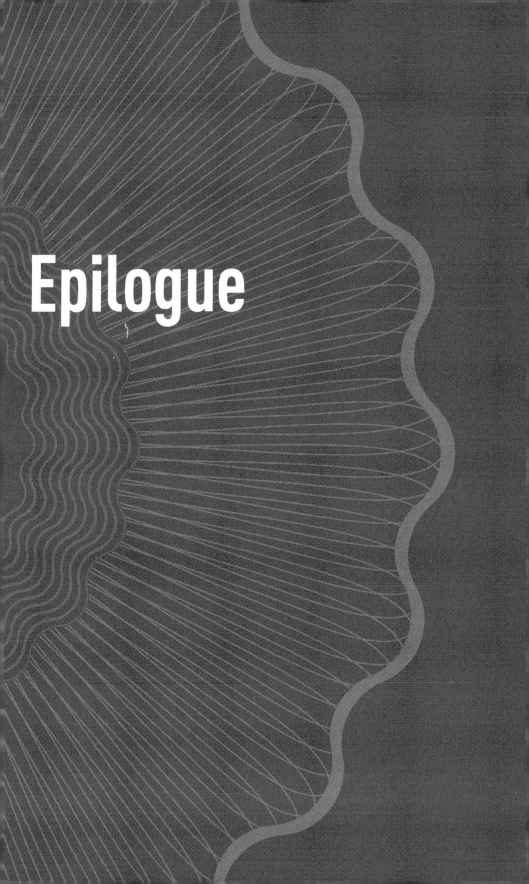

Epilogue

JD000000000

Themis was at a fixed point in the EU control when she suddenly became aware that a hushed silence had enveloped the terminal. It was a Saturday – one of the busiest days at the airport. She looked at the other positions and saw that only her colleagues rostered to occupy the other fixed points – the medical desk, fast track, and the control point for non-EU passengers – were at their posts. There were no other officers at the control because there were no passengers to be seen anywhere. Out of nowhere, two armed police officers appeared, followed closely by a tall, elegant woman carrying a briefcase. The trio approached Themis' desk.

'The Home Secretary is going to pass through your desk', one of the police officers informed her.

'OK', Themis replied.

'Hello, how are you?' asked the Home Secretary.

'I'm fine, thank you, Mrs May', Themis said, as she scanned her passport.

MAY / Theresa Mary / GBR /

'It's very quiet here today', she said.

'It is, yes', said Themis with a smile. *And the reason it's so quiet is because security has made all the commoners stay on their planes so that you can have the arrivals hall to yourself,* she thought, holding

back a chuckle at her observation. 'Welcome. Have a great afternoon', she wished.

'Thanks. You too. Have a great day at work', replied the Home Secretary politely, taking her passport from Themis.

A few moments after this brief encounter, Themis began to hear the sound of passengers rushing through the corridors again. It felt like an approaching tsunami – a still calm, followed by a mighty wave of travellers pouring in from all sides.

'What did she say, Themis?' asked her manager, dashing out from the watch house.

'Just that the control was very quiet', replied Themis.

'And what did you say?' he asked.

'I told her the truth. I said that this place is normally chaos on Saturday afternoons, but that someone had obviously arranged for all the other poor devils to be locked up on their planes until she'd gone', joked Themis, standing up from her position at the desk.

'You said what?' cried her manager.

Themis smiled.

'Just joking, chief! Of course, I didn't say that. Don't panic!'

***

Themis smiled as she remembered her encounter with Mrs May. A few years had passed since that day. They had been in Glastonbury for a couple of days, and on this summer morning, they had decided to climb Glastonbury Tor, also known as the sacred hill of Avalon. According to Celtic mythology, the Tor is one of the entrances to the Kingdom of the Fairies. In ancient times, the region was known as the Isle of Avalon. They climbed all the way up and gazed at the beautiful view from the summit. Standing alone at the top of the hill were the remains of St Michael's church, all that was left after an earthquake had mostly destroyed it in the twelfth century.

'Mummy, where's our house?' asked a small boy.

'You can't see it from here', replied Themis. 'Maybe Daddy knows what direction it's in', she said, looking at Matt with a smile.

Matt walked towards one of the compass points built on top of the Tor, and, taking the child in his arms, pointed out, 'Our castle is that way'.

A heavy fog came over them, covering almost everything. From a distance, only the Tor could be seen.

'Daddy, we're in heaven!' said the little boy.

This place really was paradise on earth.

***

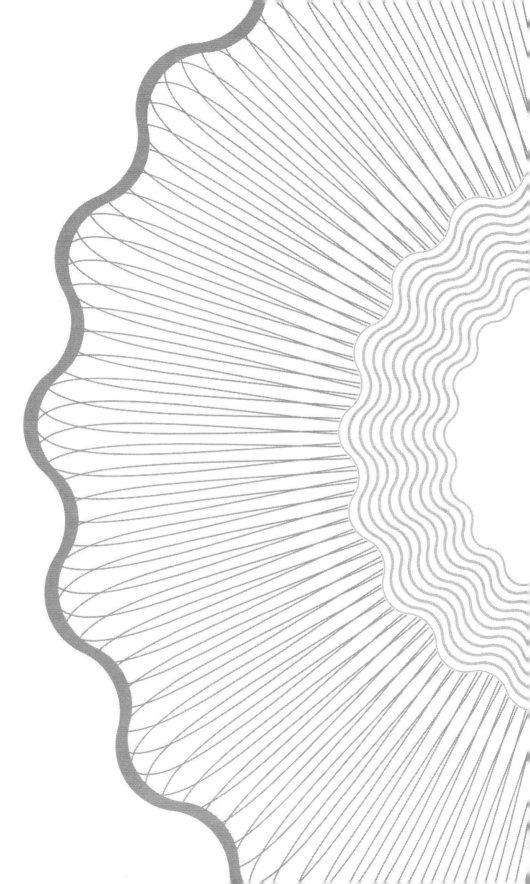

Printed in Great Britain
by Amazon

61003453R00136